Dark As Coal
Tiffany Casper

As If…
(Prelude to Zagan MC)
Book 2

Copyright © Tiffany Casper 2024

All rights reserved. No part of this publication may be reproduced, distributed, or transmitted in any form or by any means, including photocopying, recording, or other electronic or mechanical methods, without the prior written permission of the publisher, except in the case of brief quotations embodied in critical reviews and certain other noncommercial uses permitted by copyright law. Any references to historical events, real people, or real places are used fictitiously. Names, characters, and places are products of the author's imagination.

Blurb

Club girls never get their happily ever after.

It was a known fact.

However, for the men of Zagan MC, they didn't give a damn.

Only they didn't realize the battle that they would need to win.

Their hearts.

Because a girl didn't wake up and declare she was going to be a club girl.

This is Adeline & Coal's story.

Playlist

Rumor – Lee Brice

Soulshine – The Allman Brothers

Just Hold On – Savannah Dexter & Adam Calhoun

Mmm… – Laura Izibor

Zagan MC

Asher – President

Whit – Vice President

Priest – Enforcer

Creature – Enforcer

Rome – SGT at Arms

Pipe – Secretary

Irish – Road Captain

Trigger – Treasurer

Charlie – Tech

Coal – Icer

Stoney – Patched Member

Piney – Patched Member

Tide – Prospect

Fresno – Prospect

Table Of Contents

Dark As Coal

Copyright © Tiffany Casper 2024

Blurb

Playlist

Zagan MC

Table Of Contents

Prologue

Chapter 1

Chapter 2

Chapter 3

Chapter 4

Chapter 5

Chapter 6

Chapter 7

Chapter 8

Chapter 9

Chapter 10

Chapter 11

Chapter 12

Chapter 13

Epilogue

A Note From The Author

Other Works
Connect With Me

Prologue
Adeline

I couldn't help the smile that came across my face this morning as I pulled out of the clubhouse and headed to school.

My freaking jaw was starting to hurt.

How that man could say little to no words, and still completely mesmerize me, I had no freaking clue.

But he did all of that and then some.

That ever-present saying that actions speak louder than words could never be truer than when I was with Coal Matthew Adams.

With just that on my mind, I knew nothing was going to bring down the high I had going on today.

Not any of the kids that would be walking through those doors and having the mentality that they weren't going to do a thing I asked of them today.

Not creepy McPeterson, our janitor, and his wandering eyes and the licking of his lips when he sees a woman with a nice round ass.

Shiver.

Why that shiver?

Because he looked like a cross between *Grandpa Munster* and *Steve Buscemi.*

Steve Buscemi is the man who played the serial killer in the movie *Con Air.* You know, the one that sat playing with a *Barbie* doll with that little girl? Yeah, enough freaking said.

That thought was wiped from my mind when I glanced at the clock and moved to the door of my classroom.

I was ready.

I was prepared.

Any minute now, I would see my teaching assistant leading the kids from the lunchroom where they waited until the first bell of the morning sounded.

I had just gotten into place when my phone vibrated with a text.

Knowing they wouldn't be here for a few minutes longer; I pulled my phone from my dress. Yes, my pretty, mauve-colored dress that sat just below my knees had pockets.

Pockets!

I had this same dress in six other colors because of the pockets. I loved it.

Coal – *You're free tonight. Family dinner.*

Not even the text I just received was going to dampen my mood.

Nope.

Negative.

Not after the events of last night and again this morning… twice.

It didn't even bother me that he had yet to kiss me or let me kiss him. Nope, it didn't. Because after that man has had me in positions that even some Playboy Bunnies wouldn't want to be in, I didn't complain.

With that smile firmly on my face, I pocketed my phone, and just in time too.

Because I saw my teaching assistant round the corner with the kids.

I bumped fists with the boys and winked at the girls.

"Hey, Miss Adeline," I heard as one of my favorite students of this year came through the door.

Smiling down at her, I tapped the tip of her nose, "Good morning, Olivia. How are you?"

She scrunched her little nose and smiled, "I's good. Daddy made me blueberry pancakes this morning, and he didn't burn them this time."

Smiling, I nodded. "They do taste better when they're not burnt. I tend to agree. Now, go take your seat." I winked at her.

"Yes, Miss Adeline." I smiled when she skipped to her seat.

So far, Olivia's father couldn't cook eggs and the bacon was too crispy, but he had mastered pop-tarts and now blueberry pancakes.

Shaking my head, I watched as the last kid walked into the room, and then I closed the door.

As I walked to my desk, I did my usual speech, "The best-ever kindergarten class is now in session. Who's ready to have some fun?"

At once, they all clapped and nodded.

Climbing onto the edge of my desk, I called out, "Okay, for two points towards the magical chest this Friday, who can tell me what number this is?" I asked them as I held up seven fingers.

Mindy, my teaching assistant, had her eyes on the kids and caught the first one that raised their hand. She called out, "Ben?"

He smiled, showing a missing front tooth, and said, "Seven."

I smiled, "Right on, Ben."

We had a mini-board with all the kids' names on it and a table of sorts. At the top of the board, we had the day's Monday through Thursday. The top five students with the highest number of points got to raid my magical chest.

What it really was, was a small chest I picked up for a song. It was filled to the brim with little party favors, knick-knacks from the dollar store, and odds and ends from mom-and-pop stores in our town.

See, I did this, because the first year I started teaching, I had two boys, two twin boys. And after the fourth week of them coming to school in dirty clothes, the same clothes they had worn for three days, and never complaining, never not eating all their food, and being amazing kids, I reached out to a friend of mine.

She had informed me that sadly, they were the youngest of seven children and money was extremely tight because their father had been killed when he was working on a pipeline.

After my childhood, I knew what it meant when someone said the money was tight, oh how I knew.

Thankfully for those twin boys, they had brothers and sisters, and a mom that loved them fiercely, unlike I had.

But…. I bet you're wondering, why the hell would a kindergarten teacher be a club girl?

Yes… I said a club girl.

It was a long story.

And I guess my story starts at the age of five.

Yeah.

Five.

Well… technically, that was as far back as I could solidly remember.

I learned that when the men came, I was to flip the lock on my bedroom door, go to my closet, flip my little lamp on, and lock that door, too.

And in the morning, I would have to grab the medical bucket, as my mother called it, go into her room, and clean her up.

The sight of blood and vomit stopped making me squeamish by the time I turned six.

When I turned eight, I hadn't made it to my bedroom in time.

Thankfully, the man who had come that night didn't like little girls.

However, the man that came when I was nine and had kicked in my bedroom door, and my closet door… he did.

My mother had sat there on our old, dilapidated couch while pushing a needle in her vein as that man did unspeakable things to me.

And I hated her.

After a child goes through having to learn how to hand wash their clothes for school in a kitchen sink.

After a child learns they can get food from dumpsters on the weekends to hold them over until free breakfast and lunch at school.

After that child knows that while everyone is excited for Christmas break and seeing all the marvelous things Santa Claus brought them, that child is just praying that the lock on their bedroom door will hold.

That child doesn't cry when they find their mother unresponsive on the couch that morning.

They don't cry when the cops show up.

Nor do they cry when they watch their mother being covered up with a sheet and taken from the trailer.

Not even when they are placed in home, after home, after home, all so those people can get checks to feed their drug habits and make it look like they are taking care of the children in their care without doing it.

And when I was fifteen and moved into my final home, we had a neighbor.

I watched as our neighbor beat the shit out of the man who he had just seen spit on me where I lay curled up in the grass behind the house with my underwear around my ankles, my body blue and purple already.

Before that man could take me to the hospital, he had called someone, and a black van came, then a couple of men loaded the unconscious man into the back of it and sped away.

The foster family I was with got a verbal warning from our neighbor.

Thankfully, that warning held true.

No other men came to the house.

And for what he had done for me, being the first person to have my back and to care, on the day I turned eighteen, I gave him one of my kidneys.

As I lay in the hospital bed after reacting badly to the surgery, it was to find the same man, our neighbor, Piney, holding my hand.

Once he made sure I was awake and lucid, he lowered his voice, softening it, "Owe you a marker. No other person on this planet have I ever met would have come to the hospital on their eighteenth birthday and donated me, me of all fucking people, a kidney."

"That was payback," I told him with a smile. Not even recognizing my own voice.

He shook his head, "No, darlin' girl. What was payback was making my meals and cleaning my house, even though I told you, you didn't need to do that shit."

I sighed. Over the past two years, I learned that once Piney had something on his mind, there was no talking him out of it, and I knew that when he continued, "Still owe you a marker. You call it in whenever you need it. Okay?"

I sucked in a deep breath, let it out, and then nodded.

I took in his worn down, cracked face, the mangy beard that didn't know whether it wanted to be a riot of wire spring curls, or be completely straight, right as he said, "Now, what I'm about to offer you doesn't count for this marker."

Once he made sure he had my eyes, that was when Piney, a member of Zagan MC located in Fulton, Mississippi, rocked my entire world.

"Darlin' girl, the way I see it, you got this light. It's so bright it's unreal. You got a few choices, no matter what you choose, I'm gonna back you. No matter what."

Once I nodded, he laid them out.

"First, I got money. I'll help you get on your feet. I'll have your back." Immediately, I shook my head at him in the negative.

I might be damaged and used goods, which was the only thought I learned to never voice to Piney again after he sat me down at his kitchen table and ranted and raved for three straight hours.

I wasn't damaged. Nor was I used goods. No, what I was, was an angel sent to earth to shine so brightly that people needed to wear ten pairs of sunglasses just so they could look at me.

But even though I thought that about myself, except for the angel part, I saw what taking money from people did to a person. Boy, did I see it, and I had vowed that I wouldn't be like my mother.

No matter what life threw at me.

He sighed, "I know. I know. Second, if you want to be able to make your own way and have your own shit, we got something called club girls. You sign on for three years, you've got a roof over your head, and food on the table, and we cover all expenses for your education. And I want you to know, had our tech guy look into shit. Proud of you. Saw that you took college courses at the library, with a little help from the club, and in a year, you can be a teacher. So, think about what grade you wanna teach."

Even though I didn't know what a club girl was, he had me at making my own way and having my own shit.

Now, I know what you're thinking; why would a girl who had been through what I had could ever dream of being a club girl?

Simple, once Piney explained to me what a club girl was, he had gotten on the phone with the President of Zagan MC, and they brokered a deal.

I was going to be the only club girl who had the right to tell the brothers no.

And if they disrespected it, the President was going to give them the beating of their life.

It was later in the day when someone knocked on the door.

That was also the day I met Asher, the President of Zagan MC.

And it was also the day that the biggest man I had ever seen walked in behind Asher.

And I kid you not, the big man hunched his shoulders to make himself look smaller. He knew. He knew what had happened to me, and he had made sure that he showed me he wouldn't harm me.

Yes, he showed me that.

I learned a long time ago that actions speak louder than words.

And… it was that afternoon I felt down to my marrow that I had met the most important person in my life. The person that had the name Coal stitched onto his leather kutte.

He was the someone I would fall for the very first time he smiled at me.

That smile… it was a lady killer.

And the first time I heard his laugh, granted it had taken me seven months to hear it, and longer for other people, that was when he pulled my heart from my chest, and placed it in his body, firmly inside of his own heart.

Shaking my head out of my thoughts, I held up another number, and the day really began.

Chapter 1
Coal

Walking down the steps of the clubhouse, I was silent on my feet.

Everyone else sounded like a herd of elephants was going down them, but not me.

After everything I've been through, you learn to be silent on your feet.

But alas, I didn't want to end up with my head in a bottle for the rest of the day, so I tossed those thoughts out of my head.

I've been sober for three years.

And I don't plan on going down that dark path.

Not when I knew that if she ever saw that part of me, the light in her eyes that I strived to protect… would diminish.

Once I reached the bottom stair, my boot landing on the concrete floor, I tried like hell not to let the vision before me take my mind to a place it didn't need to go to.

To the woman that I needed to set free.

However, every time I thought about it... I realized I had no control.

Fucking none.

And it made it even worse anytime I saw the love between Pipe and Gabby.

Just like right freaking now.

Which instantly had my mind going back to that day... three years ago.

***

Around the old oak table that held our club insignia, a black dragon, with its wings spread out, its arrow-tipped tail ready to stab anyone that dared him harm, we were all deciding the best way to take out an MC that seemed to grow too big for their britches.

In other words, they acted like they had bigger balls than they actually had.

Normally, church was mandatory, however, even though it was, special circumstances made it possible for you to miss it without being fined a grand.

And the member that was missing was one of our oldest ones.

Piney was in the hospital on dialysis and was desperately needing a kidney.

If I had a heart left in my chest, that was even remotely beating, I would feel something for the old man.

But… well… I just didn't have that organ anymore.

Or so I thought… and that thought was erased from my brain an hour later after Asher's phone rang.

We weren't like other clubs; we didn't put our cells in a box outside of church.

We had tried that. Once.

And only once.

Some boy thought it would be okay to grab Stella's bottom when she was in the fifth grade. Stella… well… Stella didn't put up with that shit.

She had throat-punched the boy.

It wasn't until two hours later, once church had ended, that he called the school back.

And let me tell you something, that throat punch was the least of what the parents had to worry about.

Asher held up his hand as he took the call.

He let out three words once he listened to the caller, "Well, fuck me."

We all watched as he listened to whatever else was going on.

Then he stood up from his chair, looked at me, and said, "You're with me. Need your gut reaction to a person if I'm going to do what Piney just asked of me."

At my nod, he banged the gavel.

Within minutes, we got on our bikes and then headed to the hospital.

As we were walking in, Asher laid shit out for me in a low tone, "Piney just got out of surgery, and like the fool, he is, when he learned that the person who donated him the kidney had a bad reaction to the anesthesia, he got up from his bed and headed to the person's room."

I nodded, waiting for him to finish because I knew there was more to this story.

But he didn't finish. Not yet anyway.

When we made it to the elevator, the moment the doors closed he explained further, "You remember a couple of years ago, the teenager who was his neighbor that got raped and Piney beat the absolute fuck out of her rapist?"

At my nod, his words floored me, "That teenager just turned eighteen this morning, and she was the one who donated him the kidney."

I let his words process through my brain and all I could think was, holy fucking shit.

I didn't say it though, words were useless. It was your actions that spoke for you.

He saw it on my face, though, and therefore he nodded.

When the doors opened, he looked at the screen showing what floor we were on, then he looked at the nurse that was about to step onto our elevator and asked, "Darlin', you mind grabbing the next one?"

She looked at our kuttes, the whites of her eyes getting brighter with how wide her eyes were, and then she swallowed, nodded, then stepped back.

The doors closed again, and Asher mumbled, "Didn't need anyone hearing this shit and need you to know the rest. Piney plans to offer her money to help her get on her feet, but he told me he knew she wouldn't accept that. Then he asked if we could make her a club girl, but that she would be the only girl that had the power to tell anyone no. And I offered that if they didn't listen to her, I would beat the lights of them."

That was when Asher's phone sounded; he pulled it out and read the screen, then pocketed it. "She agreed to be a club girl."

I lifted my chin at him in acknowledgment and followed him off the elevator once we made it to the right floor.

And knowing my size, knowing what I come across as, the moment Asher stepped through the hospital room's doorway, I followed suit but did it by hunching my shoulders to make myself look smaller.

Let me tell you something else you don't know, nor will anyone ever fucking know.

The moment I walked in behind Asher, it had taken all of my control to not bang my chest and shout to the fucking stars in the sky with one word. Mine.

Laying there in a drab white hospital gown with little blue and pink flowers on it… there was nothing that could diminish her beauty.

She had long raven black hair that looked so soft I wanted to run my fingers through it.

But what really got me were her eyes. Eyes that I've never seen on another living soul.

They were so bright, and they reminded me of cold mornings when the sky is awash with pinks, oranges, blues, and purples.

Her eyes were the color of when the pink and the purple met.

They were fucking captivating.

And if I didn't have control over my body, I would have missed her name when Piney introduced Asher and me to her.

As I took in her features, my only thought was Adeline.

Well, Adeline, I really want to see those full, cupid bow lips wrap around my cock.

You fucker.

After everything she's been through that you know about, that isn't the way to think about her.

But come the fuck on. I was a man. A red-blooded man.

There wasn't a man alive, straight, or gay, that could look at her lips and not think about them wrapping around their dick.

I shook my head and cleared it from those thoughts.

And realized something; she was holding my gaze.

That alone told me that they didn't steal her fire.

What I didn't know at that moment in time was that I was going to break my back to make sure that no one ever managed to steal her fire.

And last, it hit me… I was fucking captivated.

Then… I watched as her cheeks took on a light pink blush and then she looked at Asher, smiled, and nodded.

He winked at her, and said, "Hey, darlin'."

And no, it didn't slip my brain that she hadn't blushed. Not at fucking all.

That alone surprised me because any time a woman looked at Asher, they fucking blushed. It was the whole silver fox vibe he had going on, or so I've heard.

Then she looked back at me, feeling this, needing this, I opened my mouth, lowered my voice, and said, "Hey."

I could feel them.

Piney and Asher's stares. They knew.

I never talk.

But I just did.

To her.

She smiled shyly back at me, her cheeks taking on that light pink blush again, and whispered, "Hi."

And with that one word, with only one syllable, she slid right beneath my skin.

***

Watching Whit and Lizette up on the platform, her tits bouncing with the motion while she was riding Whit's dick had another memory slamming into me. Hard.

No, the memory didn't come because of the lust in Lizette's gaze.

Nor did the memory come from watching her bounce on Whit's dick.

No, the memory came from seeing the look on Lizette's face and recalling the look on Adeline's face, visually, as she rode me just shy of two years ago. The look of pure adoration.

She was given the option of picking anyone to help get the memory of those hands off her mind and her body.

And you could have knocked me over with a fucking feather when she had picked me.

Not only was I the biggest son of a bitch in the club, but my body was littered with scars.

My face, chest, arms, legs, back, you name a place on my body, I've got a scar as well as a story for each and every single one of them.

And when Piney had looked at her and asked why she had picked me?

She had simply smiled while clutching the bottom of her t-shirt, and said, "Because when he walked into the hospital room, he had made himself look smaller so he wouldn't frighten me. That action says more than any mere words could ever convey."

That seemed to be all there was to it, but I could see the gears turning in a few of my brothers' faces.

It wasn't until later that night after we got her settled and brought her to the clubhouse so she could finish healing that I overheard Piney asking her the real reason why.

He knew there was more to it than that.

You didn't simply pick someone to help you get over having your body violated because of one action that took place.

Her only response was, "He's got a fire in his eyes, unlike anything I've ever seen before. And that fire tells me everything I need to know. Plus, those scars... he's been through a lot. Something tells me he wouldn't harm a single soul unless he was provoked. And something else tells me that once you get into his circle, it takes an act from God to get you out of that circle.

Piney's only response was to say one word, "Huh."

Fucking *huh*.

It was four weeks later after I heard that conversation that she managed to slip through.

Straight through my carefully planted explosives, the barbed wire surrounding my stronghold, through the concrete, I had caked on that particular organ that seemed to start beating to a rhythm she created.

I remember it like it was yesterday, taking my time, something I wasn't known for doing, fucking ever, but there had just been something in her eyes.

Something that called to me, something that no matter how hard I had fought, I had been lost.

No one else knew that she owned me.

No one else knew the power she had over me.

And no one was ever going to find out, because if they did, they wouldn't see the man I am.

No, they would only have to look at the dirt underneath her shoe, and that was where they would find me.

Because all my life, that's all I've been, nothing but fucking dirt.

However, every time I looked into her eyes, I didn't feel that way.

Never did.

No, the way I felt, it was as if someone had taken the highest voltage with a cattle prod and hit me with it. Or the way your chest expands when you view the *Grand Canyon*, *Eiffel Tower*, and *The Statue of Liberty*, all for the very first time.

I shook my head from where my thoughts were headed, knowing it wouldn't do me any good.

Sitting there in the middle of the clubhouse with a few brothers, we were waiting for Asher to get done doing whatever he was doing.

I watched as a few of the club girls came walking from the back hall while rubbing sleep from their eyes.

And none of them got me to react like Adeline did.

And yeah, I'm not going to lie to you. I have from time to time sampled the offerings from the girls who wanted to be one of our girls.

But not since I laid eyes on Adeline in that hospital bed after she donated Piney a kidney and on her eighteenth birthday, no less.

Asher came down the steps then just as Whit finished with Lizette, smacked her on her ass, and then at Asher's words, "Let's ride." We all got up and headed to our bikes.

As we pulled out of the clubhouse, eleven bikes in total, we throttled up and hit the open road.

Four hours later, we had just made our drop of guns, got paid, and found ourselves back on the open road and coasting back into the clubhouse.

Gabby, Stella, Chloe, and a few other ol' ladies were in the kitchen making food as their laughter carried out of the kitchen and into the main room.

My fingers itched to text Adeline and see if she could meet me out back. And since it was outside of the clubhouse, I wouldn't be breaking a rule.

Besides, I never got enough of her, even though I knew that fucking her was all I could give her.

But just as I thought that I felt someone's hand graze along the back of my neck.

My vision blackened immediately.

Someone. Fucking. Touched. The. Back. Of. My. Fucking. Neck.

Chapter 2
Adeline

Glancing at the clock, I sighed.

Normally, I would be heading to the clubhouse, but since tonight was family dinner night at the clubhouse, the club girls weren't allowed to be there.

However, if they lived there, then they had to stay in their rooms.

And if they ventured out of their rooms, they had to have permission from Asher to do so.

He wouldn't be giving it unless it was an emergency.

And so far, no emergency had warranted any of the girls being allowed out of their rooms.

Thankfully, I didn't have that problem.

Yes, I had a room at the clubhouse, but I also had a home.

I still hated everything about my mother, but what she did for me, I couldn't hate her all that much. It happened six months after my eighteenth birthday.

I was in my room at the clubhouse doing schoolwork when someone knocked on my door.

Priest had let me know that there was this lawyer type of looking person standing outside the gate and he was asking for me.

As I walked through the clubhouse, a lot of thoughts ran through my mind as to what this could be about.

And none of those thoughts even came close to what fell out of the man's mouth. He was indeed a lawyer.

My mother had gone through something similar to me when she was younger, and just like me, she had vowed not to end up like her own mother.

However, she got hooked on drugs, and without a support system, those drugs had taken over.

But they didn't take over while she was pregnant with me, nor did they take over while she set up an account when I was only a couple of months old.

That account was where she had the child support payments placed in; it was also an account that had measures in place that I was the only one who could access it. And that wouldn't be until I was eighteen.

Also, another measure was put into place that the balance could not be revealed to anyone until I turned eighteen.

My mother couldn't access it. Ever. No matter what she did, she wouldn't have access to it.

The account had gotten a check every month for a thousand dollars. And since the account was a trust fund of sorts, it accrued interest.

My jaw had dropped when I saw the bank statement on it.

It was only after talking to Piney in detail that I came up with something I really wanted and used that money by placing a healthy deposit on a little farmhouse that sat on five acres of wooded property.

Sighing, I looked up at the clock on the far-right wall. One more hour after the parent-teacher conferences were done would I get to go home, change clothes, curl up on my white fluffy couch, have a glass of wine, and watch one of my favorite shows.

"It was great to meet you, and if you could work with him on his r's and his s's I think it will help tremendously," I told Joshua's mother.

Joshua's mother smiled at me and nodded, "Thank you for that, we will."

Once I saw them out of my classroom, I sat back down and waited for my next parents to show up.

I wasn't sure how much time had passed but when I heard, "You're Olivia's teacher?" I looked up at that voice and at the man it belonged to and nodded.

I smiled, "Yes, and you are?"

"I'm Hank, Olivia's dad." I smiled up at him, stood up, offered him my hand, and knew that he loved his daughter deeply.

Anyone who introduced themselves as someone's father, for some reason, it just didn't hit the same way it did when someone introduced themselves as someone's dad.

"I'm Miss Adeline. Please take a seat." I gestured for him to take one of the grown-up chairs that were right beside a small kiddie chair.

He looked down at it, looked at me, and quirked his brow. I chuckled, "I know. I know. They are crazily uncomfortable, but it makes the kids feel a little more grown up."

Once he took a seat, I pulled Olivia's folder out and went over things we were going to be working on and the like.

Just as I explained a few methods he could work on with her i's and her s's, he opened his mouth, and before he could get a word out, my phone rang.

"I'm so sorry, I thought it was still on silent," I told him as I reached for it, checked the display, and then bit my lip once I felt my heart flutter.

He never called when school was in session, and he only called once it was over to let me know about something. And I always tried to take his calls.

Also, why would he be calling me while they were having a family dinner?

I looked at Mr. Grant and smiled, "I know this is extremely rude of me, but I have to take this call."

When he winked and nodded, I answered the phone, "Hey, what's up?"

And the moment I heard his heavy breathing and his words, I felt my spine straighten, oh no, "Where… Are… You?"

"Parent-teacher conferences," I told him in a soft voice, knowing that was one way I could get him to calm down.

But I knew it hadn't worked, not when he gritted out, "Need… You… Here… Now."

"Okay, umm, let me see what I can do," and as I said those words, I got nothing but dead silence.

I didn't let those thoughts enter my mind.

Nope.

It wouldn't do me any good.

I went to my contacts, tapped Asher's name, and brought the phone back to my ear and before I could get out a word, he asked, "Where you at, darlin'?

I sighed, "Parent-teacher conferences, I've got," I looked at my paper and sighed, "One more to do."

Asher cursed, "Fuck. I forgot that was tonight. Okay, we will do what we can, need you to get here as soon as possible."

I nodded, "Okay, I'll do my best."

I looked at Mr. Grant, "I'm terribly sorry about that."

Placing my phone back on the table, he nodded, "Everything okay?"

I smiled, "Yeah, just a friend who's in a bind right now."

He nodded, "Yeah, I get that, I…"

Dammit all too fucking hell.

My phone rang again. Flipping the phone over, I saw it was Gabby.

Taking the call, I said, "Hey, I need to…" and nothing else came out of my mouth when I heard that growl followed by a roar so loud, I had to pull the phone away from my ear.

"What the hell is going on?" I asked Gabby.

I could tell by her voice alone that she was scared, "Adeline, you need to get here. Now. Oh. Shit."

At her words, I asked, "What?"

"He just grabbed Lizette by the throat and threw her against the wall." I gasped.

I looked at Mr. Grant, and smiled a shaky smile, "I'm so sorry, but I've got to go."

Then to Gabby, I said, "I'm leaving now. Tell Asher."

"Okay. Be careful. But please, hurry." I nodded even though she couldn't see me, then I stood up and started getting my things.

Hurriedly, I said, "Olivia is great, I know I have your email on file, so I'll send you a few more things. Thank you for coming in."

Then I looked at Mindy and said, "Can you please take care of Eli's parents? I've got to go."

She nodded quickly, "Yes, sweetie, I got them. Go."

The drive normally took me half an hour, but I made it there in twenty minutes.

I didn't even remember pulling into the parking lot, nor throwing my car in park and killing the engine.

I was out of my car and opening the front doors of the clubhouse and the sight before me had me gasping.

Dishes were strewn everywhere. Food lay in piles on the floor, a few pieces were sliding down the walls.

Tables overturned.

Drinks spilled.

Pieces of wood that had previously made chairs were scattered.

Hearing whimpers, I looked in the direction and felt my hand come up to cover my mouth.

Lizette's throat was red, and Gabby was helping her hold an ice pack to it.

"We need to put him fucking down," Trigger grumbled as he tried to get to Coal but caught an uppercut to his face.

"Fucking keep him in the corner until Adeline gets here," Asher growled out as he, too, tried to use his body to keep Coal pinned.

"Maybe I can..." Angelyn started to say.

Asher was quick to cut her off, "Fuck no. Do you want to get thrown like Lizette did, or worse? Just stay the hell back."

I was thanking the stars in the sky that I had my ankle booties on because the crunch of glass would have ripped apart the other shoes I usually paired with this dress.

Softly, I called out, "Asher?"

Knowing he had ears like a freaking hawk, I knew he could hear me over all the yelling and growling.

His head whipped in my direction, and I saw his face go from hard to soft, "Darlin', appreciate you getting here. I wouldn't have called you, but it's bad."

I nodded, as I made my way closer to him, then asked, "What happened?"

Asher ran his hand through his hair and jutted his chin in the direction of some woman I had never seen before.

She was pretty, no doubt about it, and I would kill to be able to pull off that bright red color of hair like she could.

Just as I was thinking that Asher's voice brought me back to the here and now, "She thought he was good-looking, and wanted to show her interest in him, so she ran her hand along the back of his neck." He didn't need to say anything more.

I learned to never touch the back of Coal's neck.

There was only one time I was truly afraid of Coal.

He had pinned me to the bed, wrapped his hands around my throat, and growled in my face, showing the side of himself the whole world sees, but one I've never seen before.

And there, in my face, he had snarled out, "You ever touch the back of my neck again, I'll snap your pretty fucking neck."

I looked back at Asher and asked, "Get everyone out of here?"

He looked at Coal, then back at me, "If you were anyone else, I'd tell you to fuck off and get to safety."

I smiled, and then once he had everyone out of there, I walked over to Coal.

Slowly.

The moment I made it to reaching distance, I stopped.

And waited.

And waited.

And waited.

However, the darkness in his eyes didn't lighten at the sight of me like it usually did.

I wanted to see those mesmerizing, steel-colored gray eyes.

Therefore, I pulled my teacher's voice out of my hat and tried something different.

Softly I whispered, "I before e except after c and e before n in chicken."

When that didn't resonate with him, I smiled, and then in the same tone I had used I said, "When b, e, and c, come racing after u, s, and e, always look for a between c and u because a is shaped like the biggest man bear and it will always protect the smallest ones."

Nothing changed, nothing.

Until I watched moments later, the tenseness in his shoulders started to soften.

And at the sound of that rough, dark, damaged voice, I heard one word, "Soulshine."

I closed my eyes, wanting to let the sound of his voice calling me that name wash through me.

My eyes opened slowly when I felt my body being pulled into his hard one, and as my face pressed into his chest, I asked, "What do you need?"

Against my hair, his raspy voice said two words, just two, "Your touch."

I used to wonder why he craved my touch so much, but after I spent that first night beside him in bed, I never wondered why again.

We didn't speak about that night.

Not about the nightmare he had woken up from.

Not about the location of his hand around my throat when he came to.

Nor about the slaps to his face, I had given him, trying to wake him up and loosen his hold.

Not about the tears he shed into my oversized t-shirt.

And definitely not about the way he had said he was sorry to a little boy.

Every thought I just had flew out of my head when Coal spun, lifting me up in the process, and then walked until my back was against the wall.

My legs wrapped around him, my dress moved and exposed the tops of my thighs, but I didn't care.

And then I felt him.

Felt his hardness against the place I wanted him to slide into.

Fucking perfect.

Moments later, as his lips skinned along the column of my neck, I kept my arms out at my sides, my palms flat against the wall… I tried.

Fuck, did I try.

But it felt so good.

"Coal…" I whimpered.

With that rasp I loved so much, he bit out, "You. Hold. It. In."

I bit my lip so hard I tasted blood, trying to hold it in.

"Coal…" I moaned as he held me with one hand underneath my ass, his other hand coming up, and thankfully, I had on a thin bra.

Because the moment he brushed his thumb over my sensitive nipple, he knew it without me having to say a word.

Against my mouth, he growled, "Not. Without. Fucking. Me."

And then, he no longer had that one strong hand underneath my ass holding me up.

I was on my feet, my body spun around, my back to him, my ass in the air, my hands braced on the pool table.

My panties were ripped from my body, his hard length was at my entrance, his hands were wrapped around my hips. And then… he slammed into me. Deep.

Yes.

Perfect.

Right.

There.

I moaned.

The feel of him. Stretching me. Filling me. Completing me.

"Goddamn," he gritted out as he pulled out and then slammed back inside of me.

"Yes!" I moaned.

He was moving inside my body faster, deeper, and then I felt it.

And so did he when he rasped, "Don't. You. Do. It."

I listened.

That was until he undulated his hips, hitting that spot in me that had my toes curling.

I gasped, "Coal!"

He pulled out, "Almost." He thrust in. "There."

And then…. I felt him, his coming orgasm, and knew when he said, "Now, Soulshine. Fucking now."

I let it go.

Stars exploded behind my eyelids.

Hairs raised along the back of my neck.

And I lost all feeling in my body.

Just as he did, too.

There, against the back of my neck, he whispered, "Fuck me, Soulshine. Fuck. Me."

Chapter 3

Adeline

I awoke when I felt the first rays of sunlight stream through the curtains.

Blinking to clear the sleep from my eyes, it took my brain a moment to realize where I was.

And then... I smiled.

Because I recalled the memory of how we got here.

After he had fucked me against the pool table, he had lowered my dress, tagged my hand, led me to the kitchen, and pointed at one of the bar stools.

I didn't comment on his cum that was trickling down my thigh.

Because feeling him on me, there was nothing as erotic or as powerful as that.

While I sat there, he raided the fridge, made us sandwiches, and then together we ate them.

It was as we both took our first bites, that Asher poked his head in, looked at Coal, then at me, "All good?"

I smiled and nodded, "Yeah."

He lifted his chin, and within minutes the clubhouse was filling back up.

But apparently, we weren't staying here for it, and I wasn't going home, nor was I going to my room.

My hand was once again tagged, my bottom was off the bar stool, and we were headed up the stairs and to his room.

The very moment his door closed, our eyes locked, he was on me again, while whispering, "Earlier was for me. This is for you."

Yes, he knew how to fuck, and fuck well, but what he did great, was make slow, sweet love to me. He wouldn't call it that, I knew. But I damn sure did.

A smile hit my lips before I could stop it, and it was then that I felt a warm presence on my back.

And that was when my brain came online as to the position my body was really in.

That warm presence at my back was curled around mine, one strong arm was wrapped around my middle with my breast in his large hand.

His other arm… well… it was underneath my pillow.

And also… his very well-endowed cock was pressed into my butt.

But it was where his head was that was shocking to me.

On the night I touched the back of his neck after he told me that if I ever did it again, he would snap my neck, he whispered something to me. I knew he thought I was asleep, but I hadn't been.

'The moment I feel comfortable placing my face in your neck, all of me will be yours.'

His face was buried in my neck.

And I wanted to shout to the rooftops at how happy that made me. But something held me back. In sleep, yes, he was okay with doing that, but I was going to wait for him to do it when he was wide awake and full cognizant of doing the action.

Because I was here, in his room, a room I was rarely in, and because I didn't often get the luxury of sleeping beside him, not after that happened with the nightmare... I closed my eyes and prepared to snuggle deeper into him, revealing something that had never happened to me before, until my bladder made its presence known.

I cursed quietly and then wanted to ask God to remove the offending organ for taking this from me.

Damn.

Alas, unless I wanted to cross a line which would be to pee on him and do the so-called marking of territory, I needed to get out from under him.

Carefully, oh so carefully, I moved his arm, and then slowly moved out of bed.

And when I felt the bed shift when I didn't move, I froze and then let out a breath I hadn't realized I had been holding.

The shift had been Coal moving onto his back.

Standing up fully, I debated on what to do.

Yes, I needed to pee.

However, Coal's room didn't have a bathroom in it, and well, I didn't want to walk down the hall naked.

My dress… well… I couldn't wear that either.

See, after he led me to his room last night, he then proceeded to make love to me again, my dress ended up being the thing he grabbed to clean both of us off.

Yes, we were messy, but it was in our contracts we signed as club girls that allowed us to be messy.

I didn't know if other clubs did this, but ours did.

Asher knew of clubs where girls tried to trap the brothers, and he wasn't going to stand for that shit. So, he had a doctor come and implant a birth control device that would last the entire time you were a club girl. And if you extended that time frame then your implant was replaced with another.

Sure, I should make Coal wear a condom so if he got something from someone else then I would be clear. But it was the night that I chose him to be the one that night.

After we finished, he looked at me and said, "Won't risk you. Be only you."

I knew what he was saying. And I had thanked my lucky stars that night. The night I had picked right.

He knew he didn't have to worry about me, because it was again, in my contract. The club girls were only allowed to be with the brothers. You don't want to know the penalty if you break that law.

But… anyway, hoping I wasn't making a mistake, especially one that would make what happened last night and this morning of me falling asleep beside him, not being kicked out, and then waking up to him curled around me, I carefully walked over to the chair where some clothes were folded up.

Tagging a hoodie and a pair of sweatpants, I pulled them on and had to roll the band of the sweatpants four times to get them to fit. This would be good enough until I made it to the room I used when I stayed at the clubhouse for a little while.

After I used the bathroom, my stomach growled.

I headed down the steps, carefully walking down them so I didn't take a tumble because I didn't think my shoes would go well with what I was wearing, I had slipped on a pair of Coal's *Crocs*.

And then... at the sight before me, I abandoned my stomach growling and moved to help Lizette and Sutton in cleaning up Coal's mess.

But first, I wrapped my arms around Lizette, when she smiled at me, I knew that she was okay.

I hated seeing that mark on her though.

Freaking abhorred it.

But... well... did it make me a bad person that Coal would hurt anyone who tried to hurt him, but knew deep down in my heart that he would never hurt me?

Some days? Yes.

The other days? No.

With Coal's three sizes too big *Crocs* on my feet, I moved around the clubhouse helping everyone clean the place up.

Gabby came out of the kitchen with a trash bag in her hand, and then gasped once she saw me on my hands and knees, "Girl, what are you doing down here?"

I shrugged, my nerves were all over the place for what I was wearing and where I woke up this morning,

"He's asleep. And it would tear him up to see this place like this and know he was the cause."

A soft look formed on her face before she set the trash bag onto the floor, tagged the broom and dustpan and then started sweeping up the glass fragments.

Smiling, I teased, "So, what are you doing down here? This is beneath you."

She laughed softly and shook her head, "You can take the club out of the girl, but you can never take the female out of the woman."

I laughed softly and then got back to cleaning up.

We had just straightened everything up, and unable to ignore my stomach any longer, I found myself in the kitchen making breakfast.

A few of the brothers walked in then, and none of them commented on the clothes I was wearing, which I found odd, but for some reason, it didn't bother me.

It wasn't until I had just taken the last piece of bacon out of the pan that I felt the air in the room stir.

There was only one person who could cause that.

My eyes lifted to the entrance to the kitchen, I saw Coal look around and when his eyes locked on me, he did a top-to-toe inspection.

Unfortunately, I couldn't read his face.

However, I could read that slow, steady walk of his.

Slow.

Steady.

He wasn't worried.

He. Wasn't. Worried.

Perhaps…

The moment he made it to me, he looked down at me, and asked in a soft, raspy tone, "Why'd you leave?"

"Because I wanted to ask God to remove my bladder," I told him.

I watched, mesmerized as crinkles at the corners of his eyes appeared.

He had smiled.

It wasn't that brilliant smile, but hey, for a man like Coal, I would take it.

"Make me a plate?" He asked.

I nodded.

Then I made him and myself a plate, and carried it over to him, but, when I moved to go sit with Lizette, Sutton, and Angelyn, where the club girls sat, I felt him hook his finger in the pocket of the hoodie and I stilled.

Looking at him, it was to see him tilt his head to the seat next to him.

Was I going to question it?

No.

Negative.

No siree, Bob.

It was after we all ate, and I was helping wash the breakfast dishes that he asked something that had me rambling in nervousness, "Why didn't you come back to bed after you relieved that organ?"

Okay, that was funny, which caused me to chuckle, until my brain processed the first words of that question.

I bit my lip, was that an option? Umm.... Before I could fully process the meaning behind those words, my mouth started talking, "Well, when I had to pee, I couldn't put my dress back on. And I didn't want to go out in the hall naked." I watched as his eyes flared at that, but kept on talking, "So I put these things on, and got hungry. But well... I helped the girls clean up, and my stomach couldn't be ignored."

He didn't say anything.

Not when he nodded.

Not when he stepped away from me and headed out of the kitchen.

But... then... as soon as he was out of sight, I heard his voice loud and clear, "You look good in my shit."

Everything around me froze.

The few brothers that were still in the kitchen.

The girls.

Gabby.

Stella.

Even Chloe, Stella's best friend.

Before it fell, I swung back to the sink and sniffed, trying to keep that tear in.

And all around me, I heard…

"Damn." Gabby fanned herself.

Sutton sighed, "That was hot."

Priest, muttered, "Knew he had it in him."

Angelyn purred, "That man's voice."

Asher chuckled, "Making the rest of us look like idiots."

I was still in Coal's clothes as I started to put the dishes away that Angelyn had dried when she looked at me and said, "Look, I'm sorry about last night. But men like Coal are rare. And I've always wanted a man like him. I've always wanted to be there for a man like him and to just have him only want me and me alone."

"Is that the reason you wanted to be a club girl? To land him?" I asked.

She looked down at her short neon orange mini-skirt and then nodded.

I could see it.

Matter of fact I have seen it one too many times to count.

Therefore, I nodded, and then whispered, "I'm sorry."

Her head snapped up and then she looked at me incredulously, "Why in the world are you sorry?"

"Because I know how that feels. I know he will never claim me. That's not the type of guy he is." I told her, wishing I had been telling a lie. But it wasn't. Every word that had fallen from my lips had been the absolute truth where Coal was concerned.

At Gabby's gasp, we both looked at her to see her visibly sighing, "We forgot the right corner."

And it was easy to forget that corner, no one ever sat there, because it was too far from everything else.

***

I had just started on righting furniture in the corner when I heard Asher's voice and looked over my shoulder at him to see he was looking at me, "Darlin', normally I would have you stay down here and help finish cleaning up, but we got an allied MC almost here. Best you get up to Coal's room. Your room won't be safe. And we don't need a repeat of what all went on down here should he see you with another man."

Before I could say a word, Gabby ambled over to us and lowered her voice so only Asher and I could hear, "If you do that, it'll show favoritism, and it will show the other girls that if they get the attention from a brother as she has, they have a chance to land one of them. What if she stays behind the bar? We need help back there tonight because the prospects are in charge of the bar outside."

That was when Asher sighed, and ran a hand through his hair, "Fucking hell. Okay. Just for tonight, if anyone wants you, you tell them you're claimed for the night. And if they don't listen, you holler for me. Got it?"

I nodded then went to my room to change. A pair of fitted torn skinny jeans, black combat boots, and an army green fitted tank.

It was as I was headed to put Coal's clothes in his room, that he looked at me from his stool at the bar, crooked his finger at me, and when I got closer to him, he asked, "Where are you going with those?"

I smiled, "To put them back in your room before I get behind the bar."

He shook his head, "The guys are almost here, put them in your room, then get your ass behind the bar."

And I knew that either Gabby or Asher had relayed to Coal what the plan was. I also knew, that for the rest of the night, I would be questioning everything about us, that I thought I knew.

After I did that, I got my ass behind the bar.

It was hours later; I had slung a bunch of drinks when one of the guys in the Pagan's Soldiers MC, who was kind of cute if you were into that whole Playboy buck look.

You know the cross between a Ken doll and a frat boy?

His blonde hair flopped into his forehead, and not in that he just ran his hands threw it in a sexy way, when he said, "So, gotta ask. Gotta know. Don't see a property patch on you sweetheart. So that tells me your fair game."

Not wanting to piss off an allied club and knowing that Asher technically gave me the night off, I smiled at him and said, "I've been claimed for the night. And my job is behind the bar."

He had the audacity to freaking smirk, "Well, nothing wrong with that man letting that claim go since I'm only here for the night and I would look on it favorably if he let that claim go."

Before I could say anything to that, he further said, "I want to slam my dick into your tight, curvy body as I fist your hair around my fist. See you ain't claimed. What do I need to do?"

I was pretty sure that any other woman, that would turn her on, but I wasn't any other woman, and he wasn't Coal.

I didn't know that Rome had pulled his phone out and texted someone something before the man opened his mouth the second time.

Not until I heard that dark and deadly voice that belonged to one man, "Didn't she tell you she was claimed for the night?"

My head looked around the guy and there stood Coal with his arms crossed and his feet planted. But it was the expression on his face that even had me stilling. But... it was the unmistakable darkness that was overtaking his steel-colored gray eyes. Oh shit.

The frat-looking boy looked at Coal and for some reason, didn't read the pissed off expression on Coal's face. Yeah, he was stupid. Furthermore, he proved that when he said the next words, "Yeah, but she's just a club girl. She ain't got a patch on her."

Coal growled, "She doesn't fucking need one, motherfucker."

And that was when the Playboy Buck decided to stand up and get nose to nose with Coal, "You know who I am. You want to go head-to-head with the VP of an allied club over some piece of ass?"

Coal lifted one brow, "You want me to put a bullet in your brain for calling her some piece of ass?"

At Coal's words, everyone stopped moving, even the music turned down.

And that was when Asher walked over, "You want to end our alliance because you don't like being fucking told no?"

The frat-looking boy scoffed, "No. I want to end this alliance because my dick doesn't get hard for just anyone, but it got hard for the bitch…" Whatever he was about to say was ended when suddenly, Coal moved.

And when he moved… he threw a punch so hard at the man's temple that he staggered back and then dropped like a stone to the floor.

That was when Coal snarled, "She's the furthest thing from a bitch. Don't fucking speak to her again."

An older man walked over to Asher, I read the patch on his kutte that said one word, *President*, then he said, "Don't need to explain shit to me. He needs to learn. We good?"

Asher looked at Coal, but Coal was looking at me, and when he lifted his brow, wanting to know if I was good, I nodded at him.

His eyes stayed locked with mine for long moments.

Then he lifted his chin, looked at Asher, then at the other man, and nodded, "She's good. I'm good."

And with that, everyone got to moving, the frat boy was helped and moved away from the bar. The music was turned back up, and Coal took the stool the man had used, handed it to Rome, and said, "Burn that fucker."

Then without another word, he moved to the end of the bar and sat down.

Without him asking me to, I grabbed a coffee cup and filled it full of fresh coffee I had made for him.

Once I sat it in front of him, I got back to work.

And now, I was starting to wonder about Angelyn.

And I was starting to wonder if she was nothing more than a two-faced bitch, or if she wanted to be a club girl so she could land a brother.

See, Angelyn wouldn't have been accepted as a club girl if Pipe hadn't claimed Gabby and opened a slot.

And I was thinking she was two-faced because we clearly had that conversation in the kitchen and then she does this… Angelyn leaned into the bar, and asked Coal, "So, tell me, how come you don't let any of the girls near you."

He didn't react to that. I didn't think he would.

But still, sometimes the man would utter a sound, never a word, but his sounds, you got his meaning. Oh yes, you did.

And Angelyn just got growled at and showed bared teeth.

Thankfully, the bleach she obviously used didn't penetrate the roots and go into her brain.

I held back a smirk when she immediately walked away.

Chapter 4
Adeline

Over the past couple of weeks, things with Coal and I have drastically changed.

Gone was the hard man, and in its place was someone that was softening.

Softening in a way I never could have imagined.

I still have yet to be kissed by him, and I wanted it, desperately.

I wanted to feel his lips on mine.

But I learned early on to never push Coal. He would make his move when he was good and ready, and I had to honor that.

See, I no longer used my room at the clubhouse.

If I was there, I ended up in his bed every night.

Unfortunately, he had yet to stay the night at my house. But that was okay. We were a work in progress.

They say the best things come to those who wait for it, and fight like hell to keep it once they have it.

And if I ever had Coal, you best believe I was going to fight like hell to keep him.

Last night, he had to take care of something for the club.

And since they had some boys there, and I got a bad vibe from one of them, Asher had been cool with me not being there.

Therefore, as a result of his body not being beside mine, I had tossed and turned all night and ended up sleeping like shit.

Even though I was tired, I tried not to let it get me down today.

See, there were days I freaking loved being a teacher.

And then there were days when I absolutely abhorred it.

Like today.

Every single kid woke up on the wrong side of the bed this morning.

And being that most of them were either five years old or six years old, I had been wanting to pull my hair out by the time nine am rolled around.

They didn't want to learn more numbers.

They didn't want to know how to sound out words like bug, dog, dig, gig, zig, or zag.

Nor did they care about listening to me when I told them not to throw things.

And by the time lunch rolled around, eight parents had to be called due to a food fight that had been started because Jamison told Owen that his momma was nothing more than a whore.

And Owen being Owen… nobody insulted his momma.

That was the only time I smiled in the whole day.

I hadn't remembered sending a text to Coal on my way back to the classroom once the last student had been sent home.

Nor had I recalled him replying.

Nor my response to him.

It wasn't until I sat in my car in the teacher's parking lot with music playing, decompressing that there was a knock on my window.

I jumped at the sound and then felt my whole body relax when I saw exactly who it was and then I frowned.

Hurriedly, I lowered my window and asked, "Coal? Is everything okay?"

He lifted one single brow at me and asked, "You don't remember texting me?"

"Umm…" and with that, I tagged my phone from the cupholder and pulled up our text thread.

And that was when I saw it.

Me – *Would it be illegal to pull the fire alarm and send everyone home?*

Coal – *Probably. What happened?*

Me – *You know those days where you just want to crawl back in bed and cover up and tell the whole world it can go fuck itself?*

Coal – *Yeah.*

Me – *Well, put those wants into the minds of twenty-two kindergartners.*

Coal – *Shit.*

Me – *Shit is right. I would give my other kidney to be able to go home, curl up on the couch, eat Chinese food, turn my phone off, and watch reruns of Bones.*

Coal – *Tell you what. Need a day like that. I'll grab the food. Follow you home, and we'll do it.*

Me – *I could kiss you right now.*

Coal – *Lips are yours for the taking.*

And then, I held my breath for a beat, recalled what I thought about kissing him, and since he texted what he did, well, I took a cue from Coal.

I placed my phone back in the cupholder, and then looked up at him and crooked my finger.

The man didn't hesitate, to move his head in, and then, I finally had his lips against mine.

The kiss was tentative at first, but when Coal brought his hand to side of my face, angled my head, the kiss turned wild and hot. I felt his tongue swipe at my lips, they opened automatically, and then… his tongue played with mine.

The taste of him, like this. There was nothing like it.

I loved the way Coal smelled.

I love the way he tasted.

But this… well… this was my version of cocaine.

I'll never forget my first kiss and it made it all the sweeter that it was our first kiss.

Little did I know that not only was it my very first kiss… but it was his too.

He had followed me home, taken my keys from me, unlocked my door, and told me to go change while he got the food ready.

When I came out of my bedroom in a long-sleeved tee and a pair of shorts, Coal looked me up and down and then patted the couch just as his other hand grabbed the blanket I had on the back of the couch.

And for the next five hours, we both had our phones off, we ate Chinese food, and I was informed to never watch this show without him.

And after that night, as long as he didn't have something to do at the club, he was at my house, either I cooked, or he picked something up, and we watched Bones.

And yes… sometimes, we made it to my bed… but most of the time, my couch was never leaving my house. But the icing on all of that, no matter where we ended up, going hard, or fucking softly, our lips meeting started it all.

It was safe to say, I wasn't the only one addicted to our kisses.

No, he didn't stay the night, but that hadn't bothered me.

Things were going the way they were going, and I knew they were going at the speed that he wanted them to go.

As long as I had my time with him, then I was golden.

However, that first night, the cherry on top of that amazing night… It was seeing the hoodie I had worn that morning all those weeks ago, lying on my couch.

***

With my gray wool socks covering my feet, the pumpkin spice scent from my latte filling my senses along with the first day of fall I breathed it all in.

This was my favorite time of year.

Sure, there were a few holidays that took place during Fall; like Halloween and Thanksgiving, but they weren't important to me.

Watching the leaves changing, the colors in the sky changing, I couldn't explain it, but it was my favorite season.

And no, not just because it was football season.

My good mood which always took place on the first day of fall was interrupted by the sound I heard.

Or, I should say, by the sounds I heard.

Yes, I worked the so-called nine-to-five like a normal person, but on the nights, well, that was when I let my hair down and became my alter ego.

And that took place with one man and only one man.

Seeing the four bikes that were making their way up my drive I took in a deep breath.

"Hey guys, what's up?" I asked them after Asher killed his motor and then took off his helmet revealing the handsome face that sat beneath it, but he had nothing on Coal.

"We need you at the clubhouse, darlin'. Coal is on a tear about something, and he won't talk. Wasn't there. Said they tried your cell, but you didn't answer." Asher said, and I could tell that it was bad.

I sighed then shook my head, "I have to go to work."

"Know that darlin', but he's tearing shit apart. A-fucking-gain. Five brothers have already tried to get him to chill the fuck out but it's not working."

And that was when Irish took off his brain bucket as they called it and I saw the purple bruise on the right side of his face.

Sighing because I hadn't wanted to use any of my sick days, rather I was saving all of them to tack onto my vacation time. And right now, I am at three weeks of vacation time and twenty-three sick days.

Growling I grabbed my phone and called the principal, Embrey, she answered on the second ring, "Hey sweetie, what's up?"

"I've got a personal matter that I need to see to. I haven't called in or been late since I started. I'm sorry."

"Girl, you are the hardest-working person here. Take it. If you need more time off just let me know, and no, this doesn't take from your sick days."

"Thanks, boss lady." I smiled and then hung up.

"Give me five," I told Asher but judging by the look on his face I shouldn't bother and that I needed to get my ass in gear.

Running into my house, I pulled on his hoodie, grabbed my bag, took my keys from the hook, pocketed my phone, and then locked my door.

Grabbing my coffee, I raced to my truck, but heard Asher calling to me, "Darlin', it'll be easier if you get on the back of one of the bikes."

I hollered at him over my shoulder as I jumped in my truck, "Easier probably. But for his peace of mind and the mood y'all are telling me he's in; I highly doubt it."

He cursed, "Fuck. Hate when you're right. Okay, follow behind me and Pipe. Irish and Rome will fall behind the truck."

Nodding, I started my baby up.

We made it to the clubhouse in under ten minutes when it usually took twenty.

Shutting my truck off, I had just opened my door when I heard a loud boom from inside the clubhouse followed by the most guttural roar I have ever heard.

That alone had the men abandoning their bikes and racing inside the clubhouse.

Running right behind them, I didn't even notice the gravel digging into my socks.

And the sight before me had me cringing.

Couches were overturned. The big metal cut-out sign of the insignia for the club that hung off the main wall near where they held church was lying on its side halfway through the clubhouse.

I heard Angelyn before I saw her, and she was trying to get him to calm down by yelling at him, did she not realize that that wouldn't work?

Priest yelled at her, "Know you're trying Angelyn but you're only making it worse. We are waiting for someone, so just back off."

"I can't back off. He's hurting." She said as she tried to step towards Coal.

"Angelyn, know you haven't been here that long, but you need to get this. There is only one person on this planet who can talk Coal down when he gets like this. And you are not her." Pipe snapped at her.

"Well, she's not here so he must not be too important to her," Angelyn said as she snapped at Pipe who raised a brow at her.

Every man in the room chuckled, but it was Whit who said, "Yeah, you're delusional."

Whatever Whit was about to say was unsaid when his eyes landed on Asher and then they searched for me.

He smiled then, "Tell us what we need to do, doll."

I smiled at him and then looked at Coal as I said, "Get everyone behind me."

"You heard her, everyone behind Adeline," Asher called out as Coal grabbed the door to church.

And then he practically ripped it off the hinges with his bare hands and before he could throw it, I called out very softly, "Coal Baby?"

I kept my eyes trained on him.

However, we all ducked when he let go of the door… none of us noticed Angelyn creeping toward him, but he did, and we knew that when he threw Angelyn across the room like she was a rag doll.

Luckily, Irish was able to grab her so she wouldn't be harmed. Much.

I heard Asher say in a growl, "You go against one more thing I tell you and I will put a bullet right between your eyes."

Standing there in my short shorts, my knee-high wool socks, and the oversized hoodie I waited for him to look around the room.

And when he did, I called out again, "Coal Baby."

That was when his crazed eyes landed on me.

As I looked into his eyes, saw the fire in them, the heat that warned you, that if you got too close you were going to get burnt.

But getting burnt by him was something I lived for.

Craved it.

Needed it.

Stepping over the cushions that were lying on the floor, I lifted my foot to step over another one when I heard Coal growl low.

Freezing, I looked to where his eyes were trained and saw that right below where I was going to place my foot was nothing but broken glass.

Nodding, I stepped somewhere else that was clear and then looked up at Coal.

The beast was still out of him raging but it was eerily calm now.

So calm in fact, that I didn't move for a few seconds.

That was until I saw his nostrils starting to flare.

That alone got me unstuck as I continued to make my way over to him.

I stopped moving when I was ten feet in front of him.

The silly riddles I used weren't going to cut it this time. So, I had to try something I read about when dealing with someone who was in a red haze as they referred to it.

But what it really was, in my opinion, was a panic attack.

Keeping my eyes locked with him I spoke ever so softly as if I were coddling a wounded animal that wanted nothing more than to tear anything apart that got too close to it so it wouldn't get hurt again, "Breathe with me, Coal. In and out."

Taking his hand that wrapped around the door I grabbed it and placed it over my heart, "Feel this, Coal. Feel this. Feel my heart beating." As I said that I placed my free hand over his and felt his heart beating erratically.

And then I whispered the words he had whispered to me on a night when it was storming, we were lying naked in front of my fireplace, "You told me that your heart only beats for me while you were falling asleep. I didn't tell you that mine only beats for you. Feel me, Coal. Just me."

We stood there for long moments and then as I saw his whole body go lax, I smiled up at him, and winked, "Coal Baby, I took the day off. So how about you use me and let go of everything you're thinking about right now? Give it all to me Coal."

Angelyn started again with her mouth, "Now that he's calm, I'll take care of him."

Without even breaking my gaze with Coal I said as harshly as I could muster, "You try to come near him or touch him and I will fulfill the threat that Asher gave you."

She was off her goddamn rocker when she followed that up with, "Bitch, that man is mine."

And that one word, Coal tried to take his hand from mine, his dominant hand. The one he used to pull his gun, but I didn't loosen my hold.

"Has his dick ever been inside of you?" I asked her while still looking at Coal.

I heard her snap, "No, but that doesn't matter. We connect on a personal level."

Every single person in the room started laughing but Coal and myself.

"Personal level my ass. Has he ever said one word to you?" Rome asked her.

"No. But he doesn't need to." She was fucking delusional.

Then, I repeated those same words, "Coal Baby, I took the day off. So how about you use me and let go of everything you're thinking about right now? Give it all to me, Coal."

Just like that, whatever had him upset was gone because a small smile formed on his face and then before I could even blink, I was up and over his shoulder as he carried me up the stairs and to his room.

And if I had known the events that would follow… I would have made such a drastic move a long time ago.

He was thrusting in and out of me. I needed more. I needed it harder. Therefore, I moaned, wanting, needing, "Coal, please. Harder."

"Don't want to hurt you," he whispered into my neck.

I gritted my teeth, trying, trying to not let my temper explode from me. And when he pulled out and pushed into me, I lost the strenuous hold I had on it.

Then I snapped, "Then get the fuck out of me, and go find another girl you're not afraid is going to break."

He stilled, "That really what you want?"

"What I want is for you to open your fucking eyes and see me. Me. Not a woman that's three times less than your size. I want you to see my curves, see that I'm strong. I'm strong enough to take everything you give me." I snapped at him.

If it were even possible, his entire frame went even stiller.

"And here's a shocker for you. Maybe, hopefully, you can comprehend every word that's about to fall from my mouth, but basically. I. Want. You. All. Of. You. I don't want some half-ass bullshit. Been waiting my whole life for the right man to come along. And that man is on his knees behind me. Now, fucking give it all to me." I gritted out every word.

Chapter 5
Coal

With her words on repeat in my head, I hoped like fuck I wasn't about to make the biggest mistake of my life.

She wanted all of me, well, she was going to fucking get all of me.

Starting right now.

I pulled my dick out of her tight body, tore the condom off, tossed it in the waste basket, stood up, pulled up my boxers, and jeans, then pulled my boots on and snapped at her, "Get some fucking clothes on."

Then I moved to her door and waited.

She scrambled from the bed and pulled her clothes back on.

And yes, I took a moment to burn into memory the sight of her in my hoodie.

The moment she made it to me, I had her hand in mine and then was pulling her from the room.

Down the hall and into the main room.

The moment we stepped foot into it, every single pair of eyes was on us, not giving a fuck I said, "She wants all of me, so she's getting all of me. No one interferes."

And with that, I ignored the gasps of shock from the women, and the brothers that were slowly standing up to interfere. No. Fucking. Way. I pulled her out the back door and headed for the shed at the back of the property.

She didn't say a word, not asking me to slow down, and normally, I would have slowed down, not wanting to cause her any pain.

But then her words played on repeat in my head, *Been waiting my whole life for the right man to come along. And that man is on his knees behind me. Now, fucking give it all to me.*

Not once did she ask me where I was taking her.

And I knew the amount of trust she placed in me because Adeline Faye Hartman could spit out words like it was nobody's business.

The moment we reached the shed, I pulled the door open, released her hand, and slid the bookcase to the side, then I grabbed her hand, flipped on the light, and led her down the concrete steps.

I didn't bother replacing the bookshelf.

No one was going to be bothering us.

No one.

The moment we reached the bottom, the smell from the man who was tied to the chair in the center of the room hit me, but not like you would expect.

I turned my head to look at Adeline to see her with her arm over her nose and her eyes trained on the puddle beneath the man's chair.

He had pissed himself.

Well, that just wasn't good enough.

We would just have to see about that.

Because a man that can hold a little girl down and do unspeakable things to her, just pissing on himself wasn't nearly enough humiliation.

I didn't bother looking at her face.

I didn't want to see the horror there.

Instead, I walked over to the wall that housed my favorite tools.

That was when I heard the guy's whiney voice, "What are you going to do to me?"

I didn't bother replying.

People didn't get words from me.

I only talked when I fucking wanted to talk.

When it mattered.

And only to those that it mattered.

And I hoped like fuck that Adeline realized how special she was to me, and if she hadn't fully cottoned on to that fact, then she will never fully grasp what she means to me.

Therefore, without saying a word, I started working on him.

The first thing to leave his body were the fingers on the man's right hand.

The same fingers he had used to mutilate that little girl.

With that done, I decided to remove the fingers from his left hand too.

Fucker wouldn't need them after this.

Just as I attached the last wire to the man's flaccid cock, I looked over my shoulder at Adeline and said, "Now, I'm telling you. I won't be treating you like a whore. So, you want it harder, and rougher, I'll give it to you. When I'm fucking ready."

Then, I attached the wire to the battery box and smirked at the man's wails.

While that was shocking him, I stepped closer to her and whispered, just loud enough for her to hear me, "You want to be my woman, then you're going to take what I have to give you. And when I want to go slow and make love to you, you're going to take it with a fucking smile on your face. You got me?"

Her head tilted to the side, "Why a smile on my face, Coal?"

I didn't answer her, instead, I walked over to the man, removed the wire from the battery, and then grabbed my favorite knife.

Taking his cock in my hand, before I cut the fucker off, I looked at Adeline, "Because when I rip someone's throat out, I don't see it. What I see is your smile telling me, I'm fucking enough. And I need that. I need that bad."

And with that, I cut the man's cock off and smiled at cries of pain.

I never could have imagined what was about to follow.

So, when her words fully penetrated my brain, something in my chest cavity started to mend.

"So, if I were to give you that smile right now and tell you I want you to shove that amazing cock inside of me right freaking now, would that work?"

I never took my eyes off hers when I whispered, "Don't."

"Don't what, Coal? Told you, I wanted all of you. And this," she gestured with her hands to the shed we were in, "is also you. Coal, anything I can do to make what you do easier on you, then that's what I'll do."

I knew she could see the indecision in my eyes.

Before I could retort, she did it.

She bit her fucking lip and started to take her clothes off.

Before she could reveal more than a sliver of skin, I grabbed my screwdriver and jammed it into first the right eye, and then the left.

… And then I pounced.

Because I would be damned if anyone alive or dead, saw my woman without clothes on.

I will forever associate that corner of the shed with something so beautiful it will haunt my dreams for years to come.

And haunt them indeed.

It will haunt the nightmares and chase them away.

Chapter 6
Adeline

Just as I sliced the top of the tomato off for the burgers that we were grilling out later in the day, while the boys were in church when I heard, "Adeline, can I ask you for a favor?"

"Sure! Shoot," I told Angelyn with a small smile, not wanting to deal with her. Dealing with Angelyn was like talking to a toddler. Sure, I was a kindergarten teacher, but she was a whole hell of a lot worse.

I mean how many times have we had this same conversation?

How many times has she seen how Coal, and I are?

"So… I know the ins and outs of being a club girl, but umm… how do you land just one member?" I froze at her question.

What the hell? I, along with all of the other girls, have had this discussion about her after watching her for a few weeks but I didn't think she could be that stupid to come right out and ask that question, "Umm, a club girl doesn't just land a member. It doesn't work like that."

She scoffed, she freaking scoffed, "It did for Gabby. And the way Coal is with you, it's worked for you."

"Honestly, I don't know how to answer that question. I mean everyone becomes a club girl for reasons all their own. The reason I became one is different from Gabby's, Sutton's, and even Lizette's, none of us came into this hoping that we would land a brother. And if that is the reason you became a club girl, then you came into this for the wrong reason."

"That's not what… whatever… look, I want to know how Gabby landed Pipe, how you landed Coal, and how Sutton landed Irish. The other girls know that Coal only fucks you and nobody else. And as for Irish, well he only fucks Sutton unless there is a certain woman here but still. How are y'all doing it?"

She wasn't going to let the matter go, and I didn't know how to get through to her.

And I knew this to be a fact when not even three days later, Angelyn started up a-fucking-gain.

"How come none of the other men get near you?" Angelyn asked.

I felt the other girls looking at her, and they looked at me and all at once they shrugged.

"Does it not seem odd, and quite frankly unfair?" She asked the room.

Stella resumed her chopping of the peppers, while she said, "Honestly, not really. Coal's the Icer for this club for a reason. You want to see what will happen should another man go after the only woman he allows to even get near him?"

Stella paused, and then said, "And another fact, Gabby didn't land Pipe. Pipe chased after Gabby. As for Coal and Adeline, when one person completes the other, then it needs no label. And Sutton hasn't landed Irish. Even though she loves him, he takes her for freaking granted."

Honestly, I didn't even understand it fully.

And I wouldn't know until later about a conversation that took place while I had been in the hospital after giving Piney one of my kidneys.

Asher

(Three Years Ago)

"Wanna tell me why it's hands off of Adeline?" Whit asked me.

I looked at him, then took in the faces of all the brothers and realized they all felt the same way.

I sighed, then looked at Piney, seeing that look in his eyes, knowing what it meant.

That he knew Coal would take care of Adeline, and no one on this planet would do it better than him.

We both knew that.

And we knew that after neither of us had heard the man speak in all the time, we've known him, but we did in that hospital room.

I opened my mouth, knowing that Coal was getting information out of a child trafficker in his shed, therefore, he wouldn't be here for this particular conversation, "Any of you ever heard Coal speak?"

I watched their faces, some of them looked confused, some of them looked wary, but all of them shook their heads in the negative.

"Piney and I have. One time. One time when he first laid eyes on Adeline," I told them.

Priest was the first to ask, "When did he first lay eyes on Adeline?"

"Three days ago, in the hospital. She's the one who donated Piney his kidney."

It didn't take a person with the highest level of education to interpret the looks on all the men's faces.

Respect.

She just earned that in spades.

Piney looked around the room then and addressed the silent questions, "There are a few reasons why she's off-limits. The biggest one, she's not afraid of Coal. The next one, she donated her kidney to me on the day she turned eighteen."

"There's more to it. I know it." That came from Rome.

"The man that Piney beat to an inch of his life a few years ago… the reason behind it," I didn't have to say another word.

I nodded when I saw they all got it and then warned, "But this fact goes into your ears and stays in your brains, never to be fucking spoken of. I fucking mean it."

They all listened with their full attention.

"They released Piney later in the day, they held Adeline another day because she had a bad reaction to the anesthesia after Coal and I had met her. What we didn't know, that was until Piney asked me to ride with him so he could drop a bag of clothes off for Adeline, was that Coal didn't leave when we did."

I swallowed for the next words.

"Imagine our surprise to find out that Adeline had a nightmare, and further imagine our surprise when we caught sight of none other than Coal lying beside her in bed and holding her, running his hand through her hair and singing softly to her."

They all knew.

Every last one of them.

Coal didn't allow anyone to touch him. No. One.

But he let her.

Rome

I got it. I fucking got it.

I understood it.

Because for the woman that had hold of my heart, just like I could see that Adeline had hold of Coals, even when he says he has no heart.

And I knew that I would be whatever that woman needed from me.

No matter how hard it would be for me, I would fucking do it.

For her.

Trigger

Was I jealous of Coal?

You're damn right I was.

Adeline was a fucking dream.

She was sweet.

She was shy.

But the moment she trusted, she let it all out.

And nothing.

And I mean nothing could compare to that woman's body.

Everyone has a type.

You either like long hair, short hair, or no hair.

You either like a woman with melons and a great ass.

Or you were a fine lover of all thing's woman.

But any man, I don't care how much they lie to themselves in the mirror.

Every man will fall head over fucking pipes for a woman with soft hair, hair so long that you can wrap it around your fist while she sucks you off. Sucks you off as she looks up at you from an amazing pair of eyes that have no match.

Sucks you off with that perfect cupid bow mouth.

Makes you come, and then you lift the small body, flip her on her knees, place your hands on her perfect hips, and then pound into her tight body.

Yeah, I needed to stop.

I liked my face to look just like it does.

And if Coal ever learned of the thoughts, I was having… I shivered involuntarily.

Priest

I was happy for my brother.

So fucking happy I could scream it from the rooftops.

If there was any brother that deserved to be happy it was either Asher… or it was Coal.

Stoney

No one else had seen it, yet, but I did.

When someone has gone through the kind of things that Adeline had, it causes a darker part of you to be made known.

And I knew I'd seen it.

The world better watch out if anyone ever thought to hurt Coal.

Irish

Why was I taking the woman that has been there for me for granted?

And as many times as I had asked myself that singular question.

I just keep fucking doing it.

Whit

I joined the club because it was a band of brothers and no ol' ladies.

But Gabby changed that.

Now, I knew that Adeline was going to change that.

Furthermore, if Irish pulled his head out of his ass, he would be doing that with Sutton.

And… well… if Asher could get something right in his life, then he would be making the person that we all knew held his heart, finally fucking his.

And… I had a feeling that the moment I met the one, then I would be one of them, but until that day happened, I was going to keep on living my best life.

Chapter 7
Coal

Well, this was the first time I woke up before my woman.

And yes, she was my fucking woman.

Seeing her dark hair sprayed out on my pillow, the softness on her features as she still slept.

My hand was running softly along her spine, and I had a thought, a deep-rooted thought, one that caused me to want to see my mark on the back of her left shoulder.

If I told you the reason why I wanted it on the left wasn't that it would be closer to the single finger that held the one vein that led directly to her heart, it would be an all-and-out lie.

Just as I was thinking that she started to move around slowly.

My hand trailed down her spine, over the curve of her perfect ass, and then my fingers found the folds of her pussy.

Slowly, meticulously, I twirled my index finger around her clit.

However, as my fingers went to work, my eyes never left her face.

Slowly, I watched as her eyes started to open, I lived for moments like this when I had her eyes on me. Those stunning sea-green eyes I'd never seen anywhere else.

As soon as her eyes locked with mine, she whispered, "Morning."

"Morning, Soulshine," I felt my lips tip up into a rare smile. A rare smile that only she could bring out.

"Mmm, now, this is nice," she whispered as she ran her hand through my hair.

And just with that one touch, I was harder than a fucking rock.

An hour later, I was in the shower, when I heard the door open, and then close softly with a click. Hearing someone move around and then seeing the figure hop up on the edge of the counter through the shower curtain, it wasn't long before I heard, "Can I ask you something?"

Because it was her, my Soulshine, that response came quickly, "Ask me anything. Thought you knew that."

"I umm… I wasn't sure. I mean, I can tell things have changed, and I'm here for it, but…"

When she trailed off and didn't say more, I asked, "You're scared?"

When nothing but the sound of the water hitting the floor vibrated through the room, I didn't hesitate to whip the shower curtain open, step out, and cage her with my wet body at the vanity, "You listen to me. I know you know this, but now I'm going to spell it out in black and white for you. You ready?"

At her gasp, and her nod, I continued, "You are the only person on this planet that never has to fear me. There is nothing you could do or say that could ever bring me to hurt you. Emotionally. Physically. Nothing. I don't want you to be scared of me, ever. It's why I stopped drinking. It's why when I go into a rage, that my mind is only able to pick you out through a sea of red haze."

Bringing my hand up, I cupped the side of her face, and whispered, "Even if I ever wanted to hurt you, the monster inside me would never allow it."

I watched as her eyes closed, and then, I could feel it, the indecision, but my woman was strong, she was the strongest woman I had ever met.

And she showed me this when she leaned forward, pressed her forehead against mine, and whispered, "Will you tell me about that side of you?"

I kissed her nose, "One day. One day when I am strapped down, and I can't move, I'll tell you about it."

I knew she wanted to know more, but she let it be.

Softly, I asked, "So, are we good now?"

She tilted her head to the side and then shocked the shit out of me, because I've been waiting for her to ask me, and I was surprised it had taken her this long to do so. "Why do you call me Soulshine?"

I smirked, "Honestly, I'm surprised you haven't figured it out."

I lived for moments that I stumped this woman, winking at her, I asked, "Do you have your phone on you?"

At her nod, I said, "Search for the song, Soulshine by The Allman Brothers, and play it. And Adeline, need you to take the words in. Feel 'em. Believe 'em. Trust 'em."

Once she searched for the song and hit play, I stood there, uncaring that water was still dripping down my body, and I could tell, it didn't bother her either.

And then... then I watched her eyes flare, shoot to me, as the words, *Boy, in the darkness before the dawn let your soul shine.*

"That song tells me that I'm your woman," she whispered.

And my only course of action was to whisper back, "You listened right."

When I say that at my three words, she attacked me... I mean she really attacked me.

Her clothes were gone faster than I could blink, her lips were on mine, her hand was on my already hard cock, and she was guiding me into her entrance.

Her legs were wrapped around my hips, her heels digging in, pulling me closer to her, and her nails scraped my back.

The moment my cock slid into her tight heat, I lost all concentration and celebrated with her.

Yeah, she was mine.

After… we found ourselves in the shower, and the softness on her features after I washed and conditioned her hair, I couldn't stop myself from placing a kiss on her temple even if I had wanted to.

I had just stepped out of the shower, tagged a towel, handed it to her, tagged my own, and started drying off.

Once she had the towel wrapped around her, I asked, "You sure, that's all you wanted to know?"

"For now." She winked and then ran from the bathroom.

In. Nothing. But. A. Fucking. Towel.

I bellowed, "Anyone sees you like that, I'm putting a bullet in his brain, and then marking your ass."

Her following laughter was music to my fucking ears.

But the three words she said to me right before she exited my room, was the fucking bible to me, "I love you, Coal Baby."

But that didn't stop me from looking into the mirror as I dressed and thinking that I had way too much blood on my hands to ever be worthy of her.

What I didn't know, was that she had turned back because she forgot something, and apparently, I spoke those thoughts aloud.

***

There wasn't a person on this planet who could take this feeling away from me.

The feeling of that organ that rested in my chest cavity being sewn back together with little touches, little smiles, laughter, and most importantly love, and all of it from one woman.

One woman named Adeline.

Or so I fucking thought.

That was until someone pulled up outside the clubhouse after I had pressed a kiss to Adeline's temple before she headed to school.

And the man that folded out of his car… the woman that folded out of the passenger side?

Now they could do it.

They could cause me to breathe the promise I made to Adeline only an hour ago.

And that was when it hit me.

That was when the date hit me.

Fucking. Hell.

For the next seven minutes and forty-eight seconds, my brain, my body, everything about me… was frozen.

Bitch asked, "We are your parents. The least you can do is help us out?"

I didn't say anything.

Asshole said, "You're nothing but goddamned trash."

Bitch said, "I should have let that man have you when he wanted to."

Bitch said, "Everything you touch turns to filth. I should have aborted you when I found out I was pregnant with your ungrateful ass."

He was right. She was right.

So, what the fuck was I doing letting my blood-stained hands, touch something as pure and as sweet as Adeline?

Someone who shone with goodness from the very depth of her being.

Especially after what had been done to me. And what I had done.

I didn't watch as Asher, Priest, Trigger, and Whit forcefully removed the two of them from the property.

I didn't listen when they told me to shake whatever shit had spewed from their mouths.

Except when I heard Rome say, "You need to call Adeline."

My head whipped up so fast it was a wonder I didn't break something, and then menacingly I threatened, "You bother her? I'll kill you."

And with that, I headed to the shed.

Hours later, with their words running through my head, the feeling of those hands on me, the looks, the fucking touches, I couldn't beat it back.

So, I grabbed the bottle of *Jack* and took a pull from the bottle.

Followed by another.

Then another.

And then another.

I could feel the looks of the brothers on me.

But I didn't give a good goddamn.

I didn't speak.

Since I didn't normally speak, nobody caught the change in me, no one.

Or so I thought.

Someone was watching me from his stool.

Someone that had never let me down.

And I would soon find myself forgetting that fact.

I would also soon realize just how much Adeline loved me, even though she never spoke the words.

But that there was only so much she could take.

***

"I don't think I can do this anymore," I muttered into my bottle as the brothers mingled with another club that we were thinking of allying with.

Shocked that those words had even come to fruition in my brain.

Shocked that those words found themselves on my tongue.

Shocked that I found myself not regretting putting them out in the world.

And I should have been shocked that I had flinched from Adeline's touch earlier, and then I should have put a bullet in my head for causing a look of hurt, and pain to mar her beautiful features.

Alas, that was why I didn't drink.

But this day, and what else it really signified, I couldn't beat it all back.

"Holy. Fuck. Who the fuck is that? Momma slap my ass and call me yours," I heard Stud ask but paid it no mind like I always did.

"Who is she?" Stud asked again.

And yeah, he earned his name Stud.

It was a wonder at all the trash he had slid his dick into that it hadn't fallen off.

And that was when everything came online.

Because it clued me in as to who he was asking about.

Furthermore, I realized that my brothers were all looking at me.

It was that… it was the looks from all of them that clued me into who he was asking about.

I felt my fucking gut clench.

And then repeated the words I'd said to myself this very morning as I sat in that chair in my shed that was bolted to the cement floor by the drain.

She's too fucking good for me.

I don't deserve to touch her with how much blood is on my hands.

Let her go.

I locked eyes with Asher and gave him a chin lift. Because no one but Adeline knew I had made her my woman this morning.

He stared at me; it was almost as if I could read his thoughts in my head.

'Boy, you do this, you're going to fuck up.'

But I beat it back.

And didn't make another fucking move.

Asher shook his head, and I knew he was calling me a dumb fuck.

And I was. I knew I was. But everyone saw how sweet she was. Fucking one of a fucking kind.

And then there was me. Trailer fucking trash. Damaged fucking goods. A killer. Someone who had taken their first life at the age of fifteen. And then at the same age, on the same day, had taken the life of another.

"Her name is Adeline," Asher told Stud.

"Adeline. Never done a girl with that name." The fucker said with a lustful smile on his face.

As he headed over to where Adeline was swaying to the music with Gabby, Sutton, Chloe, and Stella, I bit the growl back.

Then I watched as Stud jerked his head over to where we were all leaning against the bar.

I watched as Adeline's eyes found mine, and then I saw her smile, she opened her mouth to say something but closed it when Stud whispered something in her ear.

…And I felt it.

Pain.

Sorrow.

But something occurred.

Something that I thought I was ready for, but as they disappeared from my view, not having her in my sight, I let the growl out.

As I pushed away from the bar to put a fucking stop to this shit, someone, someone who was about to be a dead man, grabbed me by the arm.

I stopped.

Looked down at the owner of the hand that was about to lose it, lifted my head, and locked eyes with my Pres., uncaring that he was my Pres., I lowered my voice to a dangerous whisper and said, "Get your goddamn hands off me.

Asher shook his head, "No. You're going to let this fucking happen. You won't make her your ol' lady, even though we all know she's yours. It's why none of the brothers will go near her."

"You're being a fucking idiot. Brother, I fucking love waking up with one woman. Then falling asleep with the same woman in my arms. No other feeling fucking like it." Pipe muttered before he took a pull from his beer.

Chapter 8
Adeline

I couldn't freaking believe it.

Not this.

This wasn't supposed to happen.

I had been putting the work in.

Slowly, at his pace.

I shook my head, no, this wasn't going to happen.

He told me I was his woman this morning. Laid it out for me. He wouldn't have done that if he hadn't meant it. Because Coal Matthew Adams doesn't say shit, he doesn't mean.

Using a move Coal had taught me, I twisted my arm out of his, spun around him, and then marched back into the main room of the clubhouse.

Seeing Coal going toe to toe with Asher should have stopped me from doing what I was about to do, but there is no greater pain than a woman with a broken heart.

When I reached him, just like all the other times when he felt me near, his head moved and then his eyes landed on mine.

I noticed Asher let go of him, my arm was coming back, and then my hand was slapping him across the face.

I watched as his nostrils flared but I didn't move, I waited until he righted his head, and locked those steel-gray eyes with mine.

"You're a fucking coward. I tell you that I love you, and then not even, not fucking even twelve hours later you're okay with some other man getting their hands on me. I heard you this morning, you know. I heard you. So, what if you have blood on your hands? I do, one week each month when my period is heavy, and I have to change out my tampons. Big fucking whoop."

"Hell, I sleep easier at night knowing about the men you go after and take down. I know that you're ridding the world of that kind of evil."

"Sou…" I held up my hand.

"No, you just lost the right to call me Soulshine. And what the fuck us up for someone being too good for another person? That's my decision. I'm a grown-ass woman. I choose who is good enough for me, and you were, you always have been, until the thought crossed your mind to let someone else put their hands on me."

Then I stepped back, looked at Asher then looked at Charlie because he would be the one to know, and asked, "How many months ago was my time as a club girl over?"

Charlie looked at me with a sad smile, and muttered, "Seven."

I watched as Coal took in that news.

And then I watched as his eyes flared.

But I kept going, "Yeah, I didn't have to sleep with anyone. I could have walked away seven months ago. But I didn't. For you. I never thought it was possible. But god damn, Coal. You would never lay your hands on me. And never, not once has a woman texted or called your phone. Not once have you come back from a run with the scent of another woman on you."

"And I know because when your cologne is two days old, it's faint. But it's there." I didn't realize I had tears trailing down my cheeks.

"After everything that happened this morning. What was that? Some kind of fucking game?" I asked him.

And when he still didn't answer me, when he stood there still as a statue, I knew, I knew. I knew what I had to do. It was time I stopped.

Fucking high time, I did.

And that was holding onto something and trying to be patient.

Fuck. That.

Then I looked over at Piney, and asked, "That marker you owe me? Calling it in."

He stood up, and immediately asked, "Whatcha need, baby girl?"

"You don't let him get near me while I pack my things, and then load them up in your truck and you take me home."

Piney nodded, "Done."

"I'll help, honey," Gabby said as she came to my side and wrapped her arm around my shoulders.

Stella stepped up, "Same.

Chloe got on my other side, wrapped her arm around my waist, and said, "You got me too."

"Come on, darling." Sutton grabbed my hand and then led me from the main room, down the hallway, to the right, and then down to the end of the hall where my room was.

And with their help, we got all my things packed up.

None of us paid mind to the crashing and breaking of things that were going on in the clubhouse.

I was so over it.

So. Fucking. Done.

Once we were finished, Sutton opened my door and then looked at the prospects that were standing there. "We've got her stuff. Piney's ready."

And with that, they grabbed my things and then circled me so no matter what Coal couldn't get to me.

I walked with them, my eyes forward, my chin jetted out. I wouldn't show him how much he broke me.

He got those tears earlier.

He wasn't going to get any more of them.

***

Once Piney set the last bag of my things on my couch, he walked over to me, and chucked me on my chin, "You gonna be alright?"

I smiled up at him and nodded, "You know me, Piney. I'm always alright. No matter what."

"Alright. Dinner next Friday?" he asked with a mischievous grin.

I nodded, "You know it."

Then I stood on my front porch as I watched Piney's taillights disappear down my drive.

Then I ignored the man on the bike at the end of my drive, turned on my heel, walked into the house, and flipped the locks, making a mental note that tomorrow, I was going to the hardware store and getting new locks. Ones that Coal couldn't break into.

I didn't cry as I took a shower that night.

I didn't cry as I combed my long black hair.

I didn't even shed a tear as I braided it.

I wasn't going to cry over him.

Fuck. That.

Well…. Someone should have told that to my dreaming state.

***

Two weeks. Three days. Fourteen hours. Seventeen minutes.

That's how long it's been since I've seen or talked to Coal.

Two weeks. Three days. Fourteen hours. Eighteen minutes.

That's how long it's been since I haven't cried myself to sleep at night.

And my girls were tired of seeing me being this upset.

The words were simple. "Fuck him and the bike he rode in on."

Only two days later as I sat at a corner bistro with my girls and saw the love in Pipe's eyes as he sat at a different table, keeping an eye on the situation, and making sure she stayed safe, I found myself wanting to take that statement and obliterate it from my brain.

Because I missed him.

I missed every part of him.

I missed the way his eyes would crinkle first thing in the morning.

I missed the way I could be washing dishes, and he would wrap his arms around me from behind, take the dishrag from my hand, and tell me to go sit my ass down.

Or how the way he would walk into the house while I was making dinner and dancing, and just stand there, leaning up against the wall, and watch me.

The moment I felt tears hitting my eyes, I shook my head and then started listening to Sutton talking about this dress she found when someone caught my attention.

"Miss Adeline!" I heard and then looked to where I heard that voice and found a smile hit my face.

Standing, I opened my arms just in time to hug her to my legs, "Hey there, superstar."

"Hey, guess what?"

I quirked a brow at her, "What?"

"Tomorrow is my birthday and Daddy is letting me get my nails did," her happy nature was just so infectious.

"Really? That's awesome!" And since we weren't in school, I wasn't going to correct her wording.

"Miss Adeline," I heard Mr. Grant say.

I looked up from Olivia's smiling face and smiled, "How are you, Mr. Grant."

The man was gorgeous in that rugged lumberjack kind of way, but he didn't make my heart go pitter-patter, "Call me Hank, please. Mr. Grant is my father."

I nodded, "Okay, but just know that on school grounds, you'll always be, Mr. Grant."

"Introduce us?" I looked over my head at the girls and nodded.

"Olivia, Hank, these are my friends, Sutton, Gabby, Lizette, Stella, and Chloe."

I looked at my girls, then gestured at Olivia and Hank, "Girls, this is one of my students and her dad."

Once the girls fully met him, he stepped closer to me and asked, "So, gotta know. That complication you were speaking about. Is it still a complication?"

Before I could open my mouth, I felt someone wrap their arm around my waist, and when I inhaled, I knew it was Gabby, "Why are you asking her that?"

"Because I would love to ask a beautiful woman out to dinner. The first beautiful woman my eyes have landed on in more than a fucking decade."

"Umm… I'm not sure," I said.

But it was Gabby who smiled, "You let us know and we will help her get ready."

I looked at her and narrowed my eyes, she leaned into me and whispered words that caused my heart to drop, "That man needs a wake-up call."

I narrowed my eyes at her, "And what if that wake-up call ends with this girl losing her daddy?"

"It won't. He won't. Because it will hurt you. I know he hurt you, honey, but that man is head over fucking boots for you." Gabby said.

Adeline hadn't seen the state of Coal. She didn't know that Pipe had trailed Coal for the past two weeks, three days, and fifteen hours. And wherever Adeline went, so did Coal.

And his bed roll on her front porch was the place he called home once he made sure Adeline was tucked safely in her house each night.

Chapter 9

Coal

Two weeks and five days, that's how long since I've felt dead inside.

To be honest, I forgot what that felt like.

Felt it for thirty-four years, all up until my eyes landed on my soul, shining her light at me from a hospital bed.

I wish I was one of those who could forget everything and anything after they've gotten so drunk they can't tell their ass from their elbow.

Sadly, I wasn't like that.

After being unable to fall asleep because flashes of the pain on her face kept me awake.

Being woken in the middle of the night, not from nightmares from my past, but the real visualization of those tears streaming down her face, I was a grumpy fucking bastard.

It took me two days to get my head back to right.

Four days for me to come to grips with what I had done.

Six days for Asher, Rome, Pipe, Piney, and even Priest, to talk some sense into me.

But never was I far from Adeline, unless we had mandatory church, or I needed to make a run when nobody else could do it.

Which included sleeping outside on Adeline's front porch with just my bedroll.

However, I had to go on a short run for the club, so I was late in getting myself into position so she wouldn't see me when she walked out of her house to check her mail at five forty-five.

But it wasn't her usual outfit I saw her in, no, in this outfit, she looked like she was about to go out. And I knew it when she climbed into her car and left.

I got pissed the fuck off. I was tired. I wanted to go to sleep.

But I couldn't fucking do that because she wasn't at home, and she wasn't safe.

It took until I realized I had zoned out before I realized I lost sight of her taillights, and by the time I got on my bike to follow her, I had no idea where she was headed to.

But I would find her.

But…. After fifteen minutes and no such luck, a thought occurred.

Ten minutes later I stormed into the clubhouse, my eyes taking in the scene, and the moment they landed on the one other person Adeline was close to, I stalked her and asked, "Where's Adeline going?"

And the words that fell from her mouth… it took everything I had to not let the monster out, "Oh, she's on a date."

I felt air filling up my lungs, "Where?"

"Umm, Coal, I think it might be best if you let this…" I growled.

She did what I wanted her to do. And that was to shut the fuck up.

I growled again, "Where?"

She sighed, ran a hand through her hair, and said, "They are at Luciana's."

I stalked out of the clubhouse, not bothering to stop when Asher called my name.

I made it to my bike, fired it up, and then sped out of the clubhouse.

With my mind made up about having a fucking talk with her, I missed the sounds of a few of my brothers' bikes starting up as well.

After I made the turn off onto Main Street, the moment I saw the blue and white striped overhang, I pulled up to the front, shut my bike off, swung off my bike, and then prowled into the restaurant.

My eyes scanned for her head of black hair. And the moment I saw it and the man that was seated across from her, I ignored the hostess and headed that way.

My fury was mounting. Mounting so fucking high, I thought I would have a stroke.

The moment I made it to her side, I growled, "Get up."

Adeline narrowed her eyes at me, she was the only being on this planet that could get away with it.

That was when I saw the dark blue flimsy crap of shit, she had on, "What the fuck are you wearing?"

She scoffed, "It's called a dress."

A dress my fucking ass, "It's called a fucking sheet. Now. Get. The. Fuck. Up."

That was when the fucker that thought it was okay to take my woman out on a date stood up and said, "Look man, I don't think she wants to go with you."

I looked at him, really looked at him.

He looked clean.

He looked like he didn't have the type of damage I had.

He could give her as many kids as she wanted.

He could give her the white picket fence.

Maybe…

Before I could let those thoughts take root, I mentally slapped myself.

Fucking stop it.

She doesn't see that.

She doesn't feel that.

She thinks I'm a good man.

She thinks I deserve her.

And because of all of that, I was using her in a way I never used a single soul.

I was using her to beat that darkness back.

But just a little bit so she would remain forever safe.

And forever safe she would be. At. My. Fucking. Side.

Then at the man, I snarled, "It wasn't your dick she was craving almost three weeks ago. It wasn't your back she placed her marks on. It wasn't you she was coming on. And it wasn't you she said I love you too."

"Well, now I can see why she would want to be with someone who wouldn't disrespect her by spilling special moments out in the freaking open." The man said.

Everything in me screamed at me to knock his teeth down his throat, but I refrained. Barely.

They knew I was close to blowing, I knew they were behind me.

After you've trained yourself to know that shit, it helps ease out the anxiety that reaches up through your spine.

"Don't fucking touch me," I growled at my brothers.

But I wasn't here for him.

I was here for her.

And fuck me, but she looked beautiful.

She didn't look gorgeous. No, she only looked like that when she first woke up in the morning.

And my stupid ass self has wasted three years not seeing that.

Well, that was fucking done.

Over with.

Never again would I be anywhere else first thing in the morning then lying right beside her.

With that in mind, I softened my tone, the one that only she ever got from me, "Adeline, let's fucking go."

"Am I yours?" God fucking damn her.

I growled, "You know what you are to me."

"Actually, I don't."

"If you don't get up, right fucking now, walk that sexy ass of yours to my bike, climb on, put on my helmet, I'm going to kill every single person in this restaurant."

She knew it.

She knew I would do it.

She had seen me do much worse.

Therefore, I saw something I've only seen one time before in her eyes, fucking defeat. But I vowed right then and there that I would make it right.

I would break my fucking back to do it.

When she stood up, I pulled my wallet out and tossed down a hundred-dollar bill, then I looked at the man as Adeline stood beside me, waiting.

"Appreciate you wanting to show her a good time. But she's mine. She's been mine. I fucked up. I admit that. But I ain't fucking up again. Least I can do is pay for your meal and hers." and with that, I placed my hand on the small of her back and led her out of the restaurant.

The moment we arrived at my bike, I handed her my helmet and got on.

As soon as she was on behind me, I started the bike up, gunned the throttle, and like a shot, we took off into the night.

She didn't speak.

Not when we went past the clubhouse.

Not when I turned left onto the dirt road that led to her house.

Once I parked in front of her house, I sat there for a moment, and then I spoke, "Know I lost the right to ask you this, but I plan on rectifying everything. Will you let me come in and explain?"

She didn't speak.

Not for long moments.

Two words, whispered into the breeze, "I can't."

The breath of air I hadn't realized I was holding was expelled out of my lungs at her words.

I nodded, "Then I'll wait. Till you're ready. But you best believe, Soulshine, I'm going to get what I want."

Again, with the silence, but I didn't push her, and I was grateful I didn't, not when she hesitantly asked, "And if you don't?"

I bit back a chuckle, "Then thankfully, I've got my bedroll. Slept there ever since you took your things out of the clubhouse. I'll keep doing it until you let me explain."

With that, she climbed off the bike without a word. But I didn't move.

I watched as she took her helmet off, and handed it to me, carefully, I took it in and still, I didn't move.

Watching her as she walked up the steps, pulled her key out, unlocked her door, stepped in, and closed it, only then did I move.

And that was to drop my head, sigh, and then whisper, "You're a god damned fool."

As I waited for her, the moment I saw her bedroom light go on, and then moments later it shut off, I knew she was in for the night, and she wouldn't be hearing me today.

Only then did I climb off my bike, tag my bedroll, and then got as comfortable on her porch as I could.

The next morning, I moved, lifted, twisted, and sighed when my back popped in three places.

The morning sun warmed my face.

Twisting my head over my shoulder, to see the door was still fucking closed, I got up, then walked to one of her rocking chairs, and took a seat.

Just as my ass landed on the rocker, I heard the lock on her front door, and then, she appeared.

Looking fucking gorgeous, and I knew she had just woken up.

The sleep from her eyes had yet to clear.

She took everything in.

The bedroll on her porch, my kutte I had rolled up as a makeshift pillow.

And when her eyes came back to me, I knew, and I wanted to shout it to the rooftops that she was giving me a chance. I knew it when she asked, "Want coffee?"

Ten minutes later I was sitting beside her on her couch, she was wearing my hoodie, a pair of short shorts, and those knee-high socks she loves so much when I started, "There's a reason I will never do ass play. And I thank you for never bringing it up."

I looked at her when I saw she was opening her mouth to speak, I shook my head once.

She got it. I knew it when she closed her mouth and then nodded for me to continue.

I turned my head back forward, focusing on a singular white brick that helped make up her fireplace.

"The first time it happened, I was six. The man placed his hand on the back of my neck and moved my body into position like I was a goddamned dog." I couldn't look at her as I got this out.

Because if I did, I would go on a murdering rampage.

I would kill anyone that got in my way.

"The next ten times it happened, I had yet to turn ten," I whispered.

I could feel her body shaking beside mine. I knew she caught on to what I was really saying.

I didn't need to explain it to her.

"And only one thing ended it all." I felt a tear trail down the corner of my cheek, but I didn't move to stop it, and neither did she, "That man." I swallowed, "That man I ripped apart limb from limb when I was fifteen. He got off on hurting little boys. He brought a five-year-old little boy to my room. He held a gun to my head and told me he wanted me to molest that five-year-old little boy."

Adeline was out of her spot on the couch, her hair whipping behind her, and then slowly I stood up, followed her, and found her retching in the toilet.

Tagging a washcloth, I ran water over it and then moved her hair out of her way and pressed it to the back of her neck.

After she was done retching, I helped her with some mouthwash, took her hand, and led us back to the couch.

But what she did next, had me blown the fuck away.

Once I sat back down on her couch, she sat down on my lap, wrapped her arms around my neck, and then locked her eyes with mine, silently telling me she had me. Silently telling me I could keep going.

Therefore, I continued, "I haven't let a single person touch me since I was fifteen, except for you. I didn't speak but maybe fifteen words max, before you. And you… damn, Sou… Adeline. You ripped apart everything I knew. And you did that with one fucking word."

And then, even though I gave her all the words, I needed to show her that I meant every word that came from my mouth.

I carefully lifted her off my lap, sat her on the couch, then I got up, and dropped to my knees in front of her.

Her eyes took in every movement, but she didn't speak. She waited.

And when I tagged her hand, took in a breath, and placed it on the back of my neck, a fresh wave of tears trailed down her cheeks.

I watched as she closed her eyes, swallowed, and then opened them, then whispered quietly, "Don't ever stop yourself from calling me Soulshine again. Okay?"

I grinned, "Yes, ma'am."

That was when I told her about my parents visiting… I didn't need to say more, because she did it for me, "I ever meet those two, I'm going to need you to find me a shallow grave. I also want Charlie to track down all the men that hurt you, so I can hurt them."

"Okay," I whispered.

"And if you ever say you're damaged, I will smack you upside your head, okay?"

I nodded. But I needed to make something known, "Now, let me be clear. Your mine. And I'm yours. That okay with you?"

"More than. But…" I pressed my finger to her lips.

Then I pulled out my phone and sent a text to Asher.

Me - *Need a property kutte made. She's mine. I'm hers. Pass that shit far and fucking wide.*

He replied instantly.

Asher - *About fucking time.*

Tossing my phone on her coffee table, I locked eyes with her once more and promised a promise I would forever uphold, "I won't fucking hurt you ever again, Adeline. Went thirty-four years without you. Had you. Lost you for two weeks and seven days. I won't fucking lose you again. I do something that makes you walk away from me, I'll end myself. Because there's no world that I ever want to exist in that you are not a part of."

"I forgive you, Coal Baby," she whispered against my lips.

Needing her.

Needing to feel her against me.

I did something for the first time in my life.

I made love to a woman.

To my woman.

Chapter 10
Adeline

I thought weeks ago that things with Coal and I had changed drastically, but I had no idea on how things could really change.

Everything but the furniture and a few pieces of clothing now had a home in my house.

If we didn't spend the night at the club, then we were in our bed at our house.

The morning after he told me everything, I pulled open my junk drawer, tagged the extra set of keys for my house, walked over to him, wrapped my hand around the back of his neck, pressed a kiss to his temple, and then I sat the keys beside his mug of coffee.

That got me those crinkles at the corners of his eyes.

Once we were both ready for the day, he walked me out to my truck so I could head to work, and when I whispered against his lips, "I love you, Coal Baby", that got me a soft smile and a wink.

But what got me the full smile, that was when I whistled at him as he walked to his bike to head to the clubhouse, "Take me to bed or lose me forever you handsome stud."

Now, we were at the clubhouse for a barbeque and then we were headed for a bike run that was raising money for a local charity. Allied clubs had been invited, including the members of Wrath MC and their ol' ladies. As well as the Immoral Saints MC but since none of them had ol' ladies, they had their eyes on some women that had been invited and brought by other clubs.

Coal was standing with Asher, Stoney, Piney, Whit, Priest, Rome, Pipe, Irish, Cotton, Garret, Xavier, Powers, Cam, Gage, Skinner, and a bunch of other men I didn't know the names of yet.

I was sitting with Gabby, Sutton, Lizette, Stella, Chloe, Angelyn, Novalie, Marley, Valerie, Miriam, Phoebe, Lucy, Sydney, Fiona, Lil, June, Michelle, Mackenzie, Harlow, Conleigh, Collins, Shiloh, and Savannah.

We were laughing about trying to see which of the guys would fall for letting us get our clits pierced and letting a man do it when a couple of the guys who wore Immoral Saints kuttes walked over to the table.

One of them, had I not laid eyes on Coal first, I would have wanted him, the name on his kutte read, Beast.

The one with the name Magnum on his kutte spoke, "Afternoon ladies. Tell me, did those fuckers create y'all in a lab. Cause goddamn y'all are fine."

We all snickered.

"So, I'm not getting filled with bullets, I'm talking to those of you without property kuttes on," and it took me a minute to realize that his eyes were locked right on me.

But before anyone could say a word, a shadow fell over me.

Titling my head back, I looked up at Coal, his frame was locked, and when he looked down at me, it was to say, "Tired of all the motherfuckers hitting on you, not knowing you're taken. That shit stops now."

Then he placed something in my lap that I hadn't realized he had been holding.

Tears hit my eyes when I realized what it was.

I didn't hesitate to stand up and slide it on, then I spun, brought my hands to Coal's face, pulled it down, and then I crashed my lips to his.

His growl, the tightening of his arms as they came around my body, my panties were instantly soaked.

When we both broke apart, it was to see Coal's eyes hot with hunger, yum.

"Are you fucking kidding me with this shit?" The man named Magnum asked with laughter in his tone.

Coal responded with two words, "Fucking nope."

Then without a word, Coal sat down in my chair and pulled me into his lap.

Irish walked over then and got behind Sutton's chair.

Asher came over then and got behind both Stella and Chloe's chairs' his arms crossed at his chest.

But something I didn't see coming, Rome walked over and got behind Collin's chair. Say what?!

Charlie said, "They called the charity run off."

"What the fuck?" Asher asked.

Cotton growled, "Why the fuck for?"

Charlie shrugged, "Bad weather rolling in, they were hoping it would hold off, but it's not."

That was when Cotton lowered his head and asked Novalie, "Now, Kitten, wanna tell me what the fuck y'all were laughing about?"

All at once we looked at each and then started laughing our asses off.

It was Mackenzie who sobered up first and said, with a straight face, and I didn't know how she managed it, "We want to get our clits pierced. Think Clutch can squeeze us all in?"

The men went silent. Deathly so.

Coal placed his hand on the side of my face and turned it, I bit my lip and then he whispered, "Fuck. No. I was your first. And I'll be your only. Ain't no motherfucker seeing that beautiful little clit but fucking me.

"Yeah, what he fucking said," Savage muttered.

A round of nods followed suit from all the men.

That was how the brothers got to talking and the women started playfully trash-talking each other about their men being the best.

Because every one of the men got into the ring that night and showed just how badass they really were.

In the end, there were more ties than anyone thought possible.

Cotton tied with Asher.

Skinner with Rome.

Knox with Tyne.

But my man, he didn't tie with anyone. Cause he made Beast fucking submit.

And the way my man celebrated? Well, I now had a fondness for making love in the rain. That storm that called the charity run off had come in just as the fights had finished.

Even though Coal made sure he covered my body with his the entire time, someone had watched.

Someone had gotten jealous… and it would be months before anyone truly realized that she hadn't been coming around the clubhouse like she had been.

And everyone knows that jealousy can make a person do stupid things… well, I figured all that bleach had finally ate her brain cells.

***

The feel of him moving started the wake-up process for me.

And damn, but he was a good man.

He wouldn't admit to it.

No one would ever say that about him.

But I did.

And I could.

Just like right now. He was moving quietly around our bedroom, softly cursing when he bumped into something that made the barest noise, trying his darnedest not to wake me up… yeah, that was a good man right there.

A thought suddenly hit me, I wanted to see my name on his skin.

I wanted to be on that space right above his heart that he's left bare.

I felt a tingle between my legs as I watched his back move, the tattoo twisting and turning with the movements. Recalling a few nights ago when I pressed kisses up and down his back as I rubbed out the muscle knots in his back.

"Coal?" I called softly.

He stopped what he was doing, which was pulling his boots on, and looked at me.

"Thank you for being quiet, but you move and I'm up. You don't have to be quiet."

He winked at me, telling me he appreciated the sentiment, and then finished pulling his boots on.

Once that was done, he strode over to me, pressed his lips to mine, and whispered, "Love you, Soulshine. Be careful going to work. See you later."

I nodded and smiled. "Love you too, Coal baby."

***

"Coal? Who do you think is going to win?" Priest asked.

Coal didn't say a word but pointed at the Falcon's logo.

"Fucker. Why do you always pick the underdog?"

Coal shrugged but didn't say anything.

Asher leaned down and whispered in Coal's ear, "You got that man pissing blood yet?"

Coal's hand tightened on my thigh, it was almost imperceptibly, but I felt it.

I knew what Coal did for the club.

How could I not when it was me that watched him strip out of the bloody clothes, place them in a black garbage bag, and then carry them out to the pit, Whit had started.

Once Coal nodded at Asher, he looked up, locked his eyes with mine, and lifted his brow.

I shrugged, took a pull from my beer, and said, "The only man's cock I want to suck is the one that removes filth from this earth. It's makes me sleep better."

The entire room went quiet. So quiet if a bike started, it would have broken the sound barrier.

And then very slowly, clapping started to fill up the room.

Piney cackled then, "Hot damn, that was a mic drop if I've ever heard one."

Something happened then, and it was something that it took me a beat to realize what it was.

Coal removed his hand from my thigh, got up, and walked outside.

The girls looked at me with pity in their eyes, but they didn't need to feel that way.

I learned that when Coal started to feel more than he could handle, he disappeared for five minutes.

I started the countdown in my head.

Four minutes and forty-five seconds later, Coal came walking through the door, locked eyes with mine, then retook his chair, tagged his beer, took a pull, and at the same time he put his hand back on my thigh. And squeezed.

I winked at him, I got you, Coal Baby."

He locked eyes with mine, and even though he never shied from telling me loved me, I could see it blazing in those steel-gray eyes of his.

Eyes I loved with every fiber of my being.

What we all missed, and I mean what we all missed, was something that I should have thought about the very day my contract ended.

And that something became a something exactly five weeks after our wedding.

Coal

Without warning, the door to church opened, and if there was one thing that could get every weapon in a room pointed at you, that was to open the door to church.

The moment I saw who it was, I was out of my chair, my body blocking hers.

I felt the guns lowering as I wrapped my hand around the side of Adeline's neck, "Soulshine, just cause you're my ol' lady doesn't give you the right to interrupt church."

I hated doing it, berating her.

But it had to be said.

Only, when I stared into her eyes, I knew that she wasn't bothered by my words.

Not. A. Fucking. Thing.

"I know. But I also know you. And I vowed on our wedding day, that I'd protect you. Protect every part of you. And I knew that if I didn't tell you this the moment it happened, and you found out I kept it to myself for even a minute longer, that it would hurt you."

I couldn't fault that logic.

And she knew it.

That was why she shot me that beaming smile, and I was a sucker for it.

Irrevocably so.

"Okay, Soulshine. You're right." I tagged her hand and started to pull her with me until she stopped me.

"Coal baby, you're not going to want to sit down."

I lifted a brow, "And why is that?"

"Because you're bound to wrap me in your arms and twirl me around and I'm wanting to have as long as I can with you, and that means you need to be able to pick me up and fuck me against the wall every chance we get because it turns me on. Like majorly turns me on. And sitting down, and then rising super-fast is only going to put stress on your knees."

And that was when Asher said in that particular tone that he used when he was getting aggravated, "Darlin', for those of us that don't get the dynamic between the two of you, other than y'all are fucking perfect for each other. Can you get to why you interrupted church?"

Adeline did nothing but smile, and then she pointed one finger at Asher and said, "Look here, you told me that when I first came here, I had nothing to be afraid of. So, don't you use that voice on me. Also, the only person in this room that will be guaranteed to walk out of here, is me."

And yes, she finished that equally true statement with her arms crossed over her chest and her eyebrow raised.

Then, I took in the eyes of everyone in the room and saw it, they knew it.

She would be the only one to walk out of this room still breathing, and not a hair on her body touched.

That was when Adeline turned to me, tagged my hand, and then placed it on the very last part of her body I expected.

On. Her. Stomach.

Thankfully, it didn't take my brain to come to terms with what she was telling me, and then, I lifted my brow at her, "You were right about everything you said earlier. Except one thing."

Her eyes twinkled and a brow lifted, "And that is?"

"You were precious cargo before you walked in this room, and you're even more precious cargo now. So, no way in hell am I going to risk anything happening to you and the baby by twirling you around."

"Okay…" and she stopped talking when I carefully lifted her in my arms and then looked at Asher.

"Anything else that needs me, it can fucking wait. Now, I'm going to carry my woman to my room, and worship her body like I was meant to do."

And that... well... that was why the music in the clubhouse half an hour later was loud and drowning out the sounds I was making my woman make.

Chapter 11
Adeline

Sitting at my desk, I logged into my computer to check my emails.

And one email... umm... had I read that correctly?

"Dear Ms. Hartman," yeah, that's me and I couldn't wait for the day to change my last name to Adams, "Last night our son swallowed a ring. We rushed him to the emergency room. The doctor said it was too low already to retrieve. Since we are going for perfect attendance with him, we want to get him into Yale, he will be at school today. But if you don't mind, can you please go with him when he needs to use the bathroom and check to see if the ring is in there? Awe, you will, thank you so much. Have a good day. Sincerely, Mrs. Edinson the IV."

It took me a moment to really take in exactly what the email said, and when it did, I tagged my phone and called Coal.

He answered on the third ring, and that told me that he was in his shed, but I would get to that here in a moment, "Yeah, Soulshine?"

"You will never believe the email I just got…" and then I read the email to him word for word.

Someone's mumbling in the background could clearly be heard, but I paid it no mind.

"You're shitting me," even he sounded exasperated which took a hell of a lot to do.

I shook my head, "Nope. Definitely not. Make me a promise?"

Immediately, he said, "Name it, Soulshine."

"If I ever turn into a mother that would make someone else take care of my child, shoot me."

"Soulshine, I won't shoot you; I'll just shoot myself, that way you will have a visual reminder."

And that ladies and gents, was how my panties got wet, and all I had to say was, "I love you, Coal Baby."

That dark rasp from his voice, "Love you too, Soulshine."

Those words from him caused my heart to skip a beat.

Just like it did every time he answered the call on the first ring, that meant he wasn't busy.

If he answered it on the second ring, it meant he was in church.

And of course, the third ring meant he was in the shed.

The fourth ring meant he was riding his bike.

And I never got to the fifth ring. Ever.

The day had been wonderful and since it was Friday, and on a certain day, I had plans.

Plans that would ensue Coal giving me that rare smile of his I adored.

And that was because I still held a secret.

A secret that no one knew but me.

Just as I was putting my bag in my car, I heard my name being called and turned around and frowned.

What was Angelyn doing here?

Come to think of it, I haven't seen her at the clubhouse as often. Granted, we had been staying at our place more, but still.

I offered her a kind smile, even though I wish I was one of those people who could pretend they didn't hear their name being called, "Hey, what's going on?"

She looked frantic when she rushed out, "I need your help. Look, my sister called me and said her boyfriend was getting violent with her. I was on my way to her, and remembered you got off around this time, and knew that it would be better to have help."

I felt for her, but I had one question, "Why didn't you tell the brothers?"

Something about this whole thing was screaming at me, but Sutton's words the other day had me rethinking. *'Sometimes the best way to get through to someone is to show them all the kindness you can muster… until you can't.'*

"Okay, I'll help you. But Angelyn, the moment we get your sister, I'm calling Coal. Okay?"

And that wasn't my only mistake of the day.

***

The moment we pulled up outside of a house, I turned to ask Angelyn if she was going to call her sister, but she was already out of her car shutting her door.

I'd learned to always trust my gut, trust it deeply, therefore, I typed out a quick text to Coal.

Me – *Track my location. I love you.*

Putting my phone in my back pocket, I got out of the car and followed Angelyn up the rickety porch stairs to a house that appeared to be in horrible shape.

Why would anyone be okay living in something that looked as though a good storm was going to knock the whole thing down?

But every thought was taken away when the door opened and before I could react, someone came up behind me and hit me upside my head with something.

The last conscious thought I had was that Coal better hurry his ass up.

And why the hell did I not stop to put my property kutte on?

***

"I helped bring her here. Now, where's my money?" That voice.

I knew that voice.

Carefully, to avoid as much pain as possible, I lifted my head.

And when my eyes locked on the woman standing there with straight long brown hair and that beauty mark on her right cheek, it took everything I had inside of me to not speak.

To not speak and tell her exactly what I thought about her.

To not speak and spew venom from my mouth.

And then as I watched the man with a weird ass blonde haircut that appeared his hair didn't know if it wanted to be a mullet or a shullet, hand her a thick wad of cash, she looked over at me and freaking smirked.

She freaking smirked.

What Cuntasourus.

Then she proved to be exactly the name I called her when she said, "It's nothing personal, you see."

Right.

I didn't say anything.

No, I let my eyes do the talking for me. Telling her exactly what I thought of her.

She was nothing but a two-faced, cum dumpster, America's Next Twat Model, bitch.

"Now, with you gone, I'll be able to make him fall for me." She was officially delusional. Straight-up delusional.

But that was when some man stepped from the hallway, pulled a cigarette pack from his leather jacket, tapped it on his palm, pulled out a cigarette, lit it, and then took a drag, and asked, "You know, no one has told me exactly who this woman is."

That was when Angelyn simply smiled, "It doesn't matter. Because she doesn't matter."

And I swear to god, I couldn't keep the words in, "Right. But I matter to *him*. You better take that money and run. Run as fast as those short-ass legs of yours can run. And hide. You better hide, you fucking cunt. Because once my ol' man learns it was you that handed me over to these men…" I stopped.

Let the silence wrap around me and then finish with, "You're going to get real acquainted with his shed. Believe me, I've seen the inside of it. I was able to walk out of there after he fucked me against the wall. But you… well… you won't be getting out of there. At least not with breath still in your lungs and blood in your veins. But hey, to each their own and all that."

No one said a word. No one.

Not when Angelyn simply huffed, flipped her hair over her shoulder, and walked out.

The same man that was smoking his cigarette stepped closer to me and asked, "So, just who do you belong to?"

I didn't say a word to him.

I just stared at him.

And then, apparently, he didn't like being ignored. And I knew that when his hand came up and then down and struck the right side of my face.

I moved my head to the side, bit my bottom lip, and then snarked, "He's going to eat you."

And when the man snarled and moved to strike me again, I still didn't say a word.

Both sides of my face were burning, but I still didn't utter a word.

Not until he did the one thing that would guarantee I would talk.

He pulled out his gun and pointed it at my stomach.

No one hurt my baby. No one.

Therefore, I then took great pride in telling him just who I belonged to, "I belong to Coal."

The man lost the anger on his face, his gun lowered slightly, and then I watched as that anger was replaced by… fear.

Chomp.

Then the man stuttered, "Your… you're telling me…. You belong to Coal?"

I nodded.

"Coal?" Was the man deaf? I said Coal.

Therefore, I bugged my eyes out at him asking me that again and nodded.

Yeah, the man knew who I belonged to, and I knew this when his voice got shaky, "Coal? The Icer for Zagan MC?"

I nodded, "Yes. I have his mark on the back of my shoulder. I was grabbed before I could put my property kutte on after I got off work."

He didn't say a word, he simply moved around me with a rush in his steps, pulled out a knife and suddenly, my hands were free.

Tiny pinpricks of pain raced up my arms and into my shoulders.

"Go. Run. Now."

The moment I stood, the door to the cabin was pushed open as five men walked into the room.

"What the fuck do you think you're doing?"

The man moved in front of me, blocking me. Protecting me?

This was a current of events I hadn't foreseen.

"Do you know who this woman is?" The man asked the five of them.

And I recognized one of them… but from where?

"She's a whore that turned my brother down. And nobody turns my brother down." And then, that was when I got it. That motherfucking frat boy wannabe.

He was a weasel.

"I get it. Okay. I do. Our brother hates being told no, and no one does it. But I want to know something first. Is there a member of Zagan MC that you're scared of? Because I can name one."

The man with black hair styled into a mohawk, crossed his beefy arms over his chest and asked, "Why are you asking me that?"

That was when Snaggletooth, stepped to the side and swept his hand up and down my body, "Because the woman y'all kidnapped? The woman behind me isn't a whore. She's an ol' lady now. And she belongs to the one man on this planet that I'm terrified of."

The man rubbed at his chin. And then he looked at me, "There's only one man's name that will have that girl getting free."

That was when I whispered, "Coal."

Immediately, the man with the black hair styled into a mohawk snapped, "Prove it. Where's her property kutte?

"She didn't have time to put it on after she got off work," Snaggletooth told them.

"Then how the fuck else is she going to prove it?" Another man asked.

That was when I groaned, I didn't have a way to prove but all I said was, "My property kutte was in my car."

"Where's your car?" One of them asked.

"That won't be fucking necessary," My head whipped around the four men that were standing there.

And I smiled. Asher.

But he wasn't the person that had my smile widening, and then even wider the moment his words sounded out in the rickety cabin, "Cause my woman doesn't have to prove jack shit to any motherfucker, but me."

But I saw it, out of the corner of my eye, someone had returned, someone that needed to no longer be breathing, and that someone was holding something black and shiny, and I felt my entire body go rock solid, but only for a moment.

When I told Coal I loved him, I promised I would always protect him.

And when I found out I was pregnant, I made a promise to our baby that I would always protect him or her.

But protecting Coal was more important to me because I knew that he would protect our baby, and me.

Therefore, I did the only thing that felt right.

I dove in front of Coal… just… in… time.

Chapter 12
Coal

I thought getting that text from Adeline was the only thing that could make my heart drop out of my chest.

But not a fucking thing compared to watching the woman that held my entire soul in the palm of her hand, dive in front of me, and her face going pale.

Without conscious thought, I moved my body to catch her.

Then I growled down in her face as I pressed my hand into the gunshot wound in the middle of her back, "You fucking little fool. Why?"

And what did she do? She fucking smiled, "Because… because I love you."

Leaning in close to her face, I whispered, "This is going to hurt you, and I'm so damned sorry."

Carefully, I lifted her into my arms and then ran from the house.

As we sped away from the house, I didn't think about the fuckers.

Nor did I think about the Pagan's Soldiers MC that was speeding past us.

And I also missed a chin lift from Tomb to Asher.

No, what I cared about…

The only thing I cared about was losing too much blood.

Hell, one drop of her blood being shed was too much fucking blood.

Within twenty minutes we were at the hospital.

I was carrying Adeline into the emergency room with the last shirt any of us had left, slowly filling with blood pressed into her back.

Asher placed his hand on my shoulder, "Coal, brother, they can't reach her to work on her."

I didn't care.

Rome cautioned, "Coal, brother, she's going to bleed out."

But it was her voice that had me responding, "Coal?"

I didn't notice the tear that slid from the corner of my eye, "Yeah, Soulshine?"

"I love you. Let them work. I'm not done living yet. I want… I… your… babies." And that was when I felt arms wrap around my body and pulled me back.

"She's coding. Move!"

And I watched. Helpless. As she was wheeled away from me.

Whoever was above, they better protect that fucking light of hers.

Because if they didn't, there would be rivers of blood.

In. A-Fucking-Bundance.

Seeing my reflection in the glass, seeing the blood on my shirt, my hands, my face, that was when I did the only thing that made any sense to me, I asked my brothers to guard the door to the operating room, and then I headed to the chapel.

Walked down to the altar, dropped to my knees… and I… fucking… prayed.

***

Seven hours later, after surgery, a blood transfusion, and a transvaginal ultrasound, everything should have been right in my world.

Our baby was still there, its heart beating strongly.

My woman was still breathing on her own. Her heart was still beating a rhythm that only I understood.

But it wasn't right in my world because my woman's eyes were not shining brightly.

She wasn't smiling while calling me Coal Baby.

No, all she was doing was lying in that hospital bed, resting, and breathing.

I had her right hand in mine, holding on as tight as I could without hurting her.

Closing my eyes, I rested my head on her thigh, took in a deep breath, and let it out.

That was when I heard the most amazing sound in the entire world, my head snapped up, and my eyes went right to her face, seeing those shockingly, mesmerizing, sea-green eyes of hers, her words, washed through me, "We've gotta stop meeting like this."

I chuckled, then stood, leaned in so my face was a breath from hers, with my hand braced beside her face, my other hand cupped her cheek, I titled my head and pressed the softest kiss upon her lips.

When we broke apart, I whispered, "Fucking missed you, Soulshine."

"Missed you too, Coal Baby." Not once did I berate her for the name, she started calling me.

I wouldn't ever do it.

Because never hearing it again from her lips had been a real possibility hours earlier.

Fuck. That.

My eyes were trained on hers, and at her words, I couldn't help but smile, that was my woman, "Umm, Coal?"

Still smiling, I asked, "Yeah, Soulshine?"

She lifted her left hand and asked, "Wanna tell me what this is on a very important finger on my left hand?"

I smirked, "What's it look like?"

That was when she smirked, "The fifth greatest thing I've ever seen?"

I lifted a brow, "Yeah, and what's before that?"

She smiled, "Well, the first greatest thing I've ever seen is your eyes. Second, it's your smile. By the way, your full-blown one is in the same running as when your eyes crinkle at the corners. Third, it's the look on your face when you come inside of me. And the fourth thing is the look in your eyes every time I tell you I love you."

"Well, that's all good, because all of it is a requirement," I stared simply, waiting for her to correctly fall into the hole she had dug herself in.

And that was when she asked, "Wanna explain that?"

I shook my head, wanting to say something first, and muttered, "Fuck. But I've missed you."

She smiled, but then lost that smile, and I knew what was coming, and I wasn't wrong. "I missed you, too. Now, explain."

Smirking, I said, "It would be my pleasure. It's all a requirement of being my wife. So, you see, since you already met 'em all by your words, what's the point in me asking you?"

And my woman who could spit words like it was nobody's business simply shook her head and whispered, "Fucking caveman."

I grinned, "Yours. All yours." I brought her hand to my mouth and kissed her knuckles.

"There's something I want to talk to you about," she said, and then still holding her hand I pressed it to the side of my face and gave her my undivided attention.

She smiled, "So when we first met in the hospital three years ago, it umm, it wasn't the first time I ever saw you."

What was she talking about? If I had seen her before that day, my entire world would have aligned much sooner.

"You were walking out of the grocery store, you had a bag of apples in one hand, and you were glaring at a woman who almost ran over you because she was too busy texting someone on her phone."

That was when my mind went back to that day, and I recalled seeing a flash of the prettiest head of her hair I had ever seen.

Now that I really thought about it, I should have known something was right in my world when for the first time in my life, someone made me want to take a second look.

And that second look, as she was getting in her car, a head of hair was all I had seen.

"I remember you. You know, the only thing I saw of you was your hair, and you were the only person in my thirty-four years of life that has ever made me want to take a second look."

***

Adeline stayed in the hospital for a week and a half.

It would also seem that something I never thought I would do… I would only do it for my Soulshine.

Because when the nurse tried to bathe my woman, I vehemently refused and did it myself. That included washing her hair and conditioning it.

I also had to think of every single gross thing I could muster when she moaned every time my fingers scratched her scalp.

And yes, I promised her I would wash her hair for her, anytime she asked.

Which she asked frequently in the following four weeks while she was healing.

But there was something behind her eyes that I couldn't make out.

I knew there was something else she wasn't telling me, but what it was, I didn't know.

And honestly, I had a feeling she didn't know what it was either.

But I put all of that to the back of my mind.

None of that was important.

Not a single bit of it was.

What was important was smiling down at my woman after she got out of the shower, her little baby bump looking adorable as I massaged lotion, hoping to prevent as many stretch marks as I could. But not for me.

Nope.

I didn't give a flying fuck about the marks.

They were fucking warrior marks as far as I was concerned, and the more of them the better.

"So, do you want to find your father? Between the two of us, our kids won't have any other family."

She smiled at me, brought her hand up, and caressed the side of my face, my head automatically pushed into her touch, loving it. Needing it. Always.

"Our baby has tons of aunts and uncles, a couple of cousins, and our baby already has a grandfather. The right grandfather. He or she doesn't need someone that knew where I was and didn't care. No, what he or she needs is to be looked upon the moment they open their eyes and see what pure love really looks like. And they will when their grandfather smiles down at them."

I was smarter than this. I really fucking was.

And my woman, seeing the weird battle I had going on in my head, smiled, winked, then unraveled the mystery.

I could have kicked my own ass for not realizing who she was talking about.

"Piney."

***

We made that known one month later at the family dinner. And yes, a family dinner that included all of our family.

That included Wrath MC and Immoral Saints. And this tradition would be carried out once a month until the end of time.

It was after we had celebrated my birthday by going on a secret mission, Adeline's words, and in the dead of night, we set my parent's trailer on fire.

Where it all had happened.

And wiped it away.

We also got the okay from her doctor, and she was able to get a tattoo.

An important tattoo that could be covered while she was at school.

A tattoo that had me feeling so full it was unreal.

Seeing my name on her left shoulder blade curled around protectively with flowers and vines.

And it was where my left hand was currently resting after Adeline returned back to my side.

Seeing Piney's face was enough to cause the corner of my lips to tip up when Adeline smiled at him and handed him the dark blue gift bag.

Even though she was mine. All mine. I still wrapped my other around her and pulled her to my front.

She had too many eyes on her.

Sure, they were my brothers, and they knew that she was mine, but still, you can't take the protection out of overprotectiveness.

Not with me at least.

Placing a kiss atop Adeline's head, our baby was moving around in her belly, all behind the safety and security my woman and I provided.

"What is it?" Piney asked my woman.

I knew she was smiling when she said, "You're harder to give gifts to than a three-year-old. Will you quit your grumbling and just open the damned thing."

"Feisty." He chuckled.

Nevertheless, he opened the gift bag, pulled out the white tissue paper, and sat it atop the table.

Then he pulled out his tissue-wrapped gift.

He checked the bag once more, then sat it on the floor.

Carefully, he unwrapped the gift, tilted his head to the side, and then opened the shirt up.

He had the back of it facing us, blocking everyone from the view of his face.

It wasn't until he lowered it that for the first time since I've known Piney, he had tears in his eyes.

What was on that black shirt in big white letters?

'Badass Grandpa

What's your Superpower?'

We all watched as Piney stood up, handled the shirt carefully, and then walked over to where we stood, and then he looked at me, "Need you to let her go for a moment."

For any other man, I wouldn't fucking do it.

But for him... he was a lucky bastard.

I couldn't hear what Piney whispered into her ear after he wrapped his arms around her, but judging by the smiles the two of them wore when he released her and she stepped back into my front, I knew that it was special.

Just then, Piney took his kutte off, and then his shirt, and he replaced it with that shirt, pulled his kutte back on, and when started to move away, my woman called out, "I've got one more gift for you, Piney. Well, it's really... a favor of sorts."

He smiled, and nodded, "Name it."

Everyone was silent for what would follow, and then... "Will you walk me down the aisle?"

He jerked his head up to me and asked, "Would it hurt the baby if I picked her up and spun her around?"

I chuckled, "If it didn't hurt the baby while she was on her hands and knees as I…" What I was going to finish saying was stopped when Adeline shoved her tiny hand over my mouth.

"Don't. You. Dare." She said through gritted teeth at me.

She was the only person on this planet who could get away with the shit she does with me.

Piney stood there, and then he got this look on his face, and I knew what was coming, and if it hadn't followed, the man would have lost an amount of respect from me.

"One condition. I get to tell the whole fucking world, you're my daughter." Piney looked down at my woman with a smile.

Adeline

"Fucking deal," I said with a smile on my face.

Then four words were whispered into my ear by Coal, four words I never could have imagined he would ask me, "Wanna go to Vegas?"

I lifted my brow at him, "Why?"

He winked at me, "Promised you, I was giving you all of me. Fucking meant that. Includes given you my last name."

"I know a guy with a jet," Fiona pipped up.

Knox wrapped his hand around Fiona's shoulders, "He owns a few of them, baby."

"Call him." Fiona clapped happily.

And that was how all of us, and I mean all of us, were Vegas-bound.

Five hours later the ladies and I hit the stores in Vegas and found the perfect little white dress that was biker approved.

And when we all stepped out of the massive limousine, I had no clue where it came from, Piney stood there with a big grin on his face.

The moment he locked eyes with mine, he called out, "My daughter's getting married today."

And yes, he walked me down the aisle, prouder than anything in the world.

Seven hours later, I was officially, Mrs. Coal Matthew Adams.

Fifteen minutes after that, while everyone stood guard, my husband did me dirty in a back alley.

Once our clothes were righted, he leaned his forehead into mine and whispered, "Hate that I can't help myself and defiled you in a back alley."

I smiled and curved my body fully into his, and there, I whispered back, "I'll do it anywhere with you, Coal Baby. It's fucking hot."

His eyes locked down with mine when he whispered, "I fucking love you, wife."

Chapter 13
Adeline

I wasn't sure what woke me up.

As hard as I tried, I couldn't bring back the dream I had.

That was until I looked up at the ceiling fan and saw a speck of dust that was made aware from the light sun streaming in through the window.

And that sprinkle of dust reminded me of something that caused everything in my body to tighten.

How I didn't wake Coal up with my anger I wasn't sure.

But I did know one thing, I knew that I was going to have that bitch found, and it was going to be me that ended her. One way or a fucking another.

And as I stood in the shower, I felt it.

"That fucking bitch," I muttered as my temper rose.

And rose.

And rose.

Just like the steam from the shower.

I was toweling off, pulling clothes on, and then I headed back to Coal's room to get dressed.

No. Wait. To our room.

Once I was dressed, I smiled as I watched Coal rousing from sleep.

I was sitting in the new blue wingback chair Coal had bought for me to rest in while I nursed our baby when I texted Gabby.

It was high fucking time that bitch got what was owed to her.

And I would be the one to deliver it.

Gabby responded immediately, then we pulled Lizette and Sutton into our text thread.

Coal

She got this look in her eye and then pulled out her phone and took a seat in the blue wing-back chair and I knew that she had figured out what was just outside her grasp, I said, "Baby?"

Without looking up as her fingers flew over her screen, she asked, "Yes?"

"What are you doing?" I asked, taking in the way the light in the room hit the diamonds on her left hand.

She shrugged as she started to read something, and then typed again, "Nothing? Why?"

"Because you normally don't ever mess with your phone when you're with me," I told her as I willed her to give me those eyes so I could see for myself what she was thinking, just like she could do with me.

"I love you, too. The girls want my help in getting breakfast started. As soon as that's done, I'll come back." She leaned in to kiss me, her lips so soft on my own.

But all too soon, she pulled back and then started for the door, but she stopped as she turned her head back to look at me, "Do me a favor?"

I nodded, "Anything."

"Don't you dare shave that beard off," she demanded while smiling as she left the hospital.

What I didn't know was that I should've gotten off this bed and followed her immediately.

That was until half an hour while we were in church as the girls got breakfast started when Asher's phone rang, since he was going over a report Charlie had handed him, he put it on speaker, "Yeah?"

"Dad, remind me to never piss off Adeline. Holy shit." I heard Stella, hell we all heard her.

"Language. And what the fuck do you mean?" He asked.

"Fucking Adeline came in here all sweet and smiles, and then the moment her gaze landed on Angelyn, she stormed over there, grabbed Angelyn by the hair, and then dragged her kicking and screaming to… oh shit. Ouch. Oh, that had to hurt."

"Stella, baby, focus, what happened?" Asher asked as we all stood up and then all as one, we started for the door.

On the way there I murmured darkly, "That crazy bitch touches her, I'll end her."

"Umm, Dad?" We all heard.

"Still here," He asked. None of us had yet to move.

No, we were taking in the remnants of a struggle.

Then... at her words, we still had yet to move, "Is there someplace you can hide the body?"

He asked one question, "Why?"

"No one, and I mean, no one hurts my man and lives to talk about it." We all heard Adeline as she stated that with zero remorse in her voice.

"Sweetie, if you kill her, it will live with you the rest of your life." That was Gabby.

"And? How would you feel if this bitch did the same thing to Pipe?" That was my woman.

Gabby again, "I know. But this will haunt you for the rest of your life."

"Fine." Adeline snarled. "Get me some rope."

"Rope?" That was Priest.

I knew where there was rope. And I knew where Adeline had taken her.

Spinning on my boot I headed outside, my brothers following me.

The moment we stepped into the shed, and walked down the steps, we all saw Angelyn bound to a chair in the middle of the clubhouse.

What was missing on Angelyn was her hair, apparently, my woman had used one of my knives.

But not just on her hair… no… Angelyn now had blood seeping through her shirt that had slashes in it.

Searching the main room, I finally spotted Adeline who had an ice pack on her right hand.

Walking over to her, her eyes locked with mine, "She was the one that shot me. I saw the gun from the corner of my eye before I moved to protect you. Her excuse was that if she couldn't have you then no one could."

And nothing could have prepared me after I pulled Adeline in my arms, when Asher called out, "If you're not a brother, and if you're not Adeline, then you need to get the hell out of here."

The women left, and then Asher looked at my woman, "You get your revenge all out of you?"

She didn't reply, not until she shook her head, stepped from my embrace, and muttered, "Not quite yet."

Every single man in the shed grunted when Adeline grabbed the biggest adjustable wrench I had and swung it at Angelyn's face as hard as she could.

The only words that fell from any of our mouths, came from Piney, "That's my fucking daughter."

Once Adeline nodded, dropped the wrench then stepped back into my arms, Asher looked at her again, "You good now?"

At her nod, he looked at me and said, "Cover your woman's ears."

I did that without hesitation.

And at once…. every brother pulled out their piece out and shot at vital points in the human body.

Fucking whoops.

***

Four hours later with one less callous bitch in the world, I sat in the media room with Adeline in my lap as everyone settled in with popcorn as Charlie hit play on his keyboard.

We had all the major parts of the clubhouse wired with cameras.

And everyone was glad that we did.

Seeing my woman hand Angelyn her ass, well there was nothing like it in the world.

"Fuck, I got a boner." Trigger said as he watched my woman throw punch after punch in Angelyn's face.

"You think I could talk you into divorcing his ass and becoming my ol' lady?" Priest said as he too adjusted his pants.

But the soft snores that filtered the room had told everyone that Adeline had missed both of those questions.

Laughing softly, I held her even closer as I watched the movie, and damn what a movie it was.

***

I had just laid Adeline on our bed when Asher poked his head in and said in a low tone, "We got visitors at the gate."

I lifted my chin, then tagged my pillow and pulled it closer to Adeline's head

Once I had her covered up and ensuring she was indeed sleeping, I made my way out of my room, down the stairs, and to the front gate.

And when I saw Tomb, the president of Pagan's Soldiers MC, I growled deep in my throat.

Fucking club politics and all that bullshit meant we couldn't touch the fuckers, not without declaring an all-and-out war.

Yes, I would have gone to war for Adeline, no fucking problem. And yes, we were a badass club. But if I could name three clubs, I knew we couldn't stand against and win, it would be Wrath MC, Immoral Saints MC, and Pagan's Soldiers MC.

But when Kodiak, tossed two heads towards my feet, I didn't move.

Nor did I move when Koffin tossed their VP's head at my feet, along with one more, I still didn't move.

Tomb lifted a brow at me, and asked, "We good?"

Every pair of eyes was on me.

I wanted to know something first, "Where are their bodies?"

"Gettin' ravaged. Don't really give a fuck. We don't mess with ol' ladies or kids. Everyone else, fucking sure."

I nodded, "We're good. But if my woman has nightmares from this, y'all better be ready."

"Expect nothing less," Tomb muttered then I watched, along with the rest of my club as all the members of Pagan's Soldiers MC climbed on their bikes and rode away.

"Sorry you couldn't get your revenge, brother," Rome said at my side.

I shrugged, "My woman is safe and happy. That's all that matters to me."

And until the day I stopped breathing, that was my number one priority.

Epilogue

Coal

One Month Later

I stared at the picture that someone captured on our wedding day.

She finally had her proof that I was in fact a human and not a robot.

The photographer I didn't know that we apparently had and on such short notice, had captured the moment when I saw Adeline in her wedding dress for the first time.

And my little minx just had to get an eight by ten printed out on canvas and hung it in the hallway so she could see it every morning, and every night.

We also prepared for the arrival of our little girl. Yes, we found out last week that we were expecting a little girl. I also made a mental note to stock up on more guns.

Because if she looked anything like her mother, I was going to need them.

Leaving the picture, I headed into the nursery to start building the crib we bought yesterday. Along with anything my woman's eyes landed on that she wanted our little girl to have.

Because what my woman wanted, she got.

And this also sparked a conversation that we should have had years ago.

But that was just me and Adeline.

And… I finally shared what I did that brought money in.

Adeline had gone to her phone after I told her and pulled up those texts.

Coal - *Getting justice.*

I was a contract killer up until the first morning when she woke up beside me in my bed at the clubhouse.

And because Charlie was a smart motherfucker and invested my money for me, I never had to work a day in my life.

And neither did Adeline.

She was so joyful that she got to be a stay-at-home mom, that right in the middle of our garage after I had told her, and after I had put my weapons in a safe, she dropped to her knees and showed me her appreciation.

Ten minutes later because my woman had an amazing mouth and I was a sucker for her, I helped her up and then proceeded to eat her out on our kitchen table.

***

I was walking beside Adeline through the early onset of snow, and laughing my ass off as she acted like a child. Sticking that delectable tongue out and trying to catch snowflakes, when I looked at the closed gate at the clubhouse.

It was to see the prospect, kneeling on the ground in front of a little girl.

A little girl in a pink flowered dress.

Everyone was behind us because we all planned to go out to eat.

It was then that the prospect took the little girl's hand in his and led her over to where we were all standing.

And the last words I ever thought were going to fall from the prospect's mouth came out, "Says she's looking for Irish."

But that wasn't the only thing that was happening that day.

Because not even two minutes later something else happened.

I couldn't fucking believe it.

Could never fucking believe it.

The man that was getting off his bike… it better be high time to rip that Nomad patch from his kutte.

And now that I had Adeline in my life.

My light.

It was okay for me to admit this.

I fucking missed the hell out of Creature.

However, that wasn't what had my full attention.

No, it was the whiteness in Adeline's face when she grabbed her stomach.

It was time.

Adeline

"Umm, your husband knows there's a bathroom in here, right?" The nurse asked as I started to feel another contraction.

"He's fine. He just needed five minutes. He'll be back."

"I swear, men. It's the women that experience childbirth. Not them. Like we can get up and move around when we have a seven-pound ball being shoved out of our vaginas."

I bit my tongue, wanting to tell her to send me another nurse.

I wouldn't stand for anyone to say one thing bad about Coal.

But then I was in the throes of another contraction, which took my breath away, but only for a few moments.

I didn't hear the door open.

I tilted my head and looked at the woman, "Are you married?"

She nodded.

"Would you trust him with your life?"

She nodded.

"Would your man kill for you?"

She hesitated, unsure, but nodded.

"Would your man torture someone but flaying the skin off their bones? And he would do that simply because someone scared you?"

Her face went pale.

I smiled, "Yeah. My man would do all of that. And he has done all of that. So, if he needs five minutes while I'm in labor because he's seconds from killing everyone in this hospital because I'm in pain and he can't do anything about it… then he's allowed all the time he needs."

The nurse didn't say anything, not when Coal appeared at my side, wrapped his hand around my throat, his fingers placed just so, so he could feel my pulse, and then he whispered, "I can't take you out in public."

I snorted. "She had no right to judge you. At fucking all."

He tightened his fingers for the briefest second, "I know. It's one of the many reasons why I love you."

I treasured those words that he spoke.

Of course, I could feel his love for me.

I felt it with every breath he took.

But when he gave me the words, it completed my world.

And my world became even more complete when I finally pushed our little girl out of me.

I will never forget the vision of Coal holding our little Leticia Gayle Adams close to his chest while he sang to her.

Five Years Later

Adeline

Of course, we would hear this kind of conversation while we were out for dinner for our fifth anniversary.

"Telling you right now girl, just like this Octopus on my forearm, I don't intend to be that for you,"

"Then what do you intend to be for me?"

"A Hugopus."

I watched the confusion morph over the girl's face.

Then I looked back at the man and saw he looked sad, "You don't get it?"

"I…" she didn't say anything more.

I looked at the man, titled my head, the thoughts running through my mind, I turned my head slowly and locked eyes with Coal.

Then slowly, I asked, "How the hell do you hug a pussy?"

At my words, Coal smirked, "Must mean you cover the pussy with your whole mouth."

"Well, that wouldn't be any fun," I muttered as I took a bite of my broccoli.

He lifted one shaped dark brow at me and asked, "How so? You love it when I…"

He trailed off as I started speaking, "Yep. You did that, you wouldn't be able to flick my clit the way you do and cause back-to-back orgasms."

"Well, shit. Fuck that." and with that, we continued eating like nothing happened.

Coal

Our precious four-year-old little Lettie asked, "Dad?"

I looked at her from my phone, "Yeah, baby?"

She lifted a tiny brow and asked, "Is Mom a badass?"

Oh hell, Adeline was going to kill me, and needing to make sure I curbed her words, I asked, "Do you want your Momma to wash your mouth out with soap? You know better than to use that kind of language."

She scrunched up her brow then, "Dad, you told me to sound out my words, and that's what's written on this case."

I looked up to see what she was holding and when my eyes landed on that particular disc I smiled, and then had to apologize to my baby, "Yeah baby, your mommy is a badass. And you are right. I did tell you to sound out your words. I'm very proud of you."

I sat my phone down on the coffee table and then took the disc from her, popped it into the DVD player, picked my girl up, and settled her on my knee in the recliner.

And then I tilted my head as I watched my little girl's face as she watched her momma go all out on the woman.

Lettie gasped, "Why did she do it?"

I waited until Lettie was looking up at me, her mother's eyes reflected back and whispered, "Because someone hurt me. And according to your Mama, no one hurts me."

"I want to be just like her. But I'm going to start listening to Mama more. I had no clue she could do all of that." I smiled down at her.

I tapped the top of her nose, "Your mommy would never hurt you, princess."

Adeline

With my arms wrapped around Coal, on the back of his bike, we both watched the young man kick ass out on the soccer field.

He would never know what my man had done for him.

But I would.

I so would.

Only… when the young man happened to look up, he stared straight at us, and I knew… I knew it then. He knew who the man at my front was.

The young man offered Coal a two-finger salute and then we both watched as he smiled wide, and then headed off to chase the soccer ball.

And if anyone ever tried to harm this amazing man of mine, then you can bet your ass, I will be as *Dark As Coal*.

Only worse.

The End.

A Note From The Author

Tiffany was born in Charlotte, NC. She will always live below the Mason-Dixon line because there isn't a place on earth like it.

She's happily married to her hubby and together they have five kids. And two dogs.

She loves reading and writing, country music, rock music, and taking random rides down back roads with the windows down and music blaring.

And yes, she swears up and down that she wanted to be born in 1960 so she could fully live in the 70's. The best things were created then.

XO Tiffany.

Other Works

Wrath MC

Mountain of Clearwater

Clearwater's Savior

Clearwater's Hope

Clearwater's Fire

Clearwater's Miracle

Clearwater's Treasure

Clearwater's Luck

Clearwater's Redemption

Christmas in Clearwater

Dogwood Treasure

Dove's Life

Phoenix's Plight

Raven's Climb

Wren's Salvation

Lo's Wraith

Falcon's Rise

Lark's Precious

Sparrow's Grace

DeLuca Empire

The Devil & The Siren

The Cleaner & The Princess

The Soldier & The Dancer

Willow Creek

Where Hearts Align

Charlotte U

Perfectly Imperfect

Imperfection is Beauty

As If...

(Prelude to Zagan MC)

Cold As Ice

Dark As Coal

Pinewood Lake

Rise

Virgin Mary's

Old Fashioned

Standalone

In Case You Didn't Know

Novella's

Hotter Than Sin

Silver Treasure

Wrath Ink

Future

Connect With Me

Facebook

https://www.facebook.com/author.tiffany.casper

Instagram

https://www.instagram.com/authortiffanycasper/

Goodreads

https://www.goodreads.com/author/show/19027352.Tiffany_Casper